New Hybrids Time Vault (Series) books I II III inclusive

Time Vault

I0567605

Nick Betar

Published by Nick Betar at LuLu

Copyright 2012-2014 Nick Betar

Contact: c/o Australia Fair post office, Australia Fair,

Qld 4215, Australia.

~~~~

ISBN: 978-0-646-94400-5

Table of contents

Chapter 1 The Vault

Chapter 2. The dig

Chapter 3. The humanoid

Chapter 4. Renee

Chapter 5. Bus to Athens

Chapter 6. Onlio's chance meeting

Chapter 7. Lorenzo's anguish

Chapter 8. Renee and Marcie

Chapter 9. Lorenzo's disparage

Chapter 10. Renee and Marcie's goodbye

Chapter 11. Renee and Lorenzo

Chapter 12. Searching

Chapter 13. The find

Chapter 14. Journey to Neru

Chapter 15. Vested interests

Chapter 16. Inquiry

Chapter 17. Awakened

Chapter 18. Recollection

Chapter 19. Callum's quest

Chapter 20. Recognition of each other

Chapter 21. Preparations

Chapter 22. Re-union

Chapter 23. Surveillance on the ground

Chapter 24. Morphed judgment

Chapter 25. Search of the vault

Chapter 26. Destruction

Chapter 27. Recorded events

Chapter 28. Celebrations

Chapter 29. Atlantis

Chapter 30. Broadcast from the heavens

Chapter 31. Renee's thoughts

Glossary of contents

~~~~

Preface

A group friend's get together on the journey that will take them to a new discovery through the vaulted passage ways of a mysterious chamber like a time capsule of space history. This will lead the characters Lorenzo and Renee to decide what they should do and that whilst in the midst a group of friend's, they should decide themselves onto the path to this magical

2

realm of another world and through their interest of archaeological discoveries and history of the area that they are drawn into before them, make this decision from a message given, "I am part of the collective of their tribe, the unconscious, we came down aeons ago and left our mark on humanity." It is to this end that this couple could now catch up on a discovery they could not have guessed at but felt with a seeming endless unerring that seems to travail this story and lure them further into, with past acquaintances and forgotten areas of their life brought into question and a re-establishing of why things can happen as they do and what we as fellow citizens on this Earth as human beings, are challenged with in one way or another as our lives prevail. This is a fiction but could well be a real and true happening, could this have happened somewhere before in the Earthly past? That's what this read will bring forth on their adventure.

Chapter 1. The Vault

Greece is an historical and mythical place that is also steeped in science through-out its history and for the archaeological discoverers in this story of the anomaly in the province of Kalambaka, in Greece is no exception and contained within this area are monasteries and caverns in this geological landscape. There is a village located five kilometres from the province, that holds the key to the paradoxical intent that this group of archaeologists to be were to experience. It was to lure and unfold to them and it will be the mysteries of space contained there. Legend has it that it has been hidden and held within a cavern and that a man named Lorenzo and his lovely fiancé to be Renee, were to experience during its discovery. He and his father were well acquainted with this history of its legend as well and here the secrets of the untimely or timely to others, opening of an ancient 'vault' that once revealed would change the passage of time for the region and eventual their world forever more.

Lorenzo is a man with an unusually checker-board life of upheavals as well as triumph and his father he believed added to this, that being to the good fortune of opportunity he and his father Onlio had with simple farming techniques and good harvests of grapes achieved much in their community over the years, though never on an industry scale, there lurked the 'time vault' legend, deep in his father's mind.

3

It was thus that Lorenzo's father Onlio retired to Athens in an apartment, what was then given to the children by his father was kept in the family, though Lorenzo was given the opportunity to keep the farm going for himself his father and the rest of the family. Having just sold the farm and his other farm in the lower crop yield areas of that settlement Onlio decided to leave Kalambaka. Lorenzo, now looking for a change as he neared the middle years of his life, remembered something in his early childhood that would take place when the myth of the 'Vault' was to be found out, this deeper lurking message. Having grown up with his grandfather and father telling him stories and disturbing occurrences around this 'time vault' and about the place but for most of the story telling the treasures there were 'fables' and not real spiritual one's. Whether this was said to protect him or not, he was not certain, this his father told him. This created in him, the obsession for Lorenzo to go to this place time and time again, over the years, sparking up interest with old friends, particularly school pals. They would find items ranging from trinket type artefacts, for example shard pieces of ceramics to finds of unusual block sized of old granite, hewn off many years ago. This obsession was to increase into an area of a simple grassed field with thickets of bush and after a day of searching for clues, turned up for more visits in this place and this is when his friend with the same interests in archaeology, began searching this avidly. They turned up a number of interesting artefacts to permanently perk his interest in the matter and to know deep down in his heart, these were no fables told as the objects took on a curiosity about them and a feeling that he was close. Lorenzo, repeated in his mind, affirmations on finding the treasure, "I will find this treasure, whatever this is, I know it's got to be here!", he would say to Renee and she was interested, though she felt she had to take a break from it at this point, she became more diverted from it and distracted by home life activities and tending to the crops on the farm. Though Lorenzo did continue this, his feelings he had were more intentioned on the home life. Prior to all this though later on in his life from when his grandfather and father had spoken of the 'time vault' and archaeology in the area, a friend of his father's who was into archaeology and connected to the olive farming practice, by the name of, Demetri and would interest him in archaeological digs or searches and was a benefit to Lorenzo's earlier experience and interest in this field of expertise. This is what got Onlio interested after his enlistment to the army and Onlio had been interested in this field since being an infantry man and sometime later in his life as a part time archaeologist. He speculated with Demitri, talking about this for hours with Demitri. "What was there? Was it a lost fortune in treasures?", he would bounce this off back and forth to Demetri between themselves and thinking about what might really be there in the area. His father would speculate at one time or another to him, as to old tombs, full of lost mysterious knowledge, he pondered continually this line of questioning, "Just what could it be and what era?"Later, Lorenzo and others joined up an archaeological group type forum with him, which included some old school friend's and he looked around at various other places. Finding bits of ceramic from the older civilizations? Close to the area of Kalambaka and once in a while a piece of metal of an unusual construct would turn up and this generated interest because it seemed to be from an unknown period in the histories past and as the metal in general was most of the time old unmarked copper coinage. He and the group contributed to the historical finds and local museums. However he pondered, "What was the significance of what his father had told him?"

They were well organised for the searches of these places, gaining permission and on this particular day, Lorenzo was whilst washing up a find of old bottles in a creek bed, not far from a place he and his companions had searched negated a furtherance to the searches and it was to this end, when an older relic turned up and it appeared to be iridescent in colour and was large with the feel and shape of a ceramic tile and he shouted to one of his companions, Janice, to look. "See if we can find another piece like it!" "Ok, sure, there is bound to be more around here I guess", flicking her eye's to the sky as if they done this routine thousands of times. Later they found another fully intact ceramic tile, this had a spider impression put into it which was equally unusual to the first tile. Remembering what his father had always told him about the spider in mythology he had uncovered himself through the years. Now for the group was not so much the tile they had found but as to the gate in through which the vault was contained, they were close!

In Lorenzo's family there were three other members, his sister, Lumina of whom accompanied him earlier on expeditions around the area and seemed very close but now was travelling through Greece as a sales representative and was hardly in touch, a younger brother, Markus, and he lived only ten kilometres away and yet seemed to Lorenzo to be a thousand kilometres. He had not kept in touch that much and the older, Tobias who was now living in America and scantly ever would be in communication with, he was truly as he saw it, the black sheep of the family. He was an outsider for his apparent comprehension of things

5

psychic and metaphysical, it was also as if he felt at times, he had another mother and father. It made him sad from time to time to think he was thinking this way. Some days he would seem very distant to them, not really interested in the past when his parents called up and it's what caused him to pick up the friend's he did, who seemed odd and uninterested in worldly events and to take up also the interest's he and they had together. These all fit into his work ethics and he in theirs He was however working at a job in his father's previous olive grove of which was run partly by his younger brother who came over to see him, being the older brother working on that farm and after mostly being run by his father, having left and moved into retirement in Athens. It was also for any family member to spend time in at the estate each with the idea that the father had planned some objective with something other than the farm.

A pattern began to emerge in all the groups searching and this included mostly local people and childhood friend's from their school days who shared this common and dark bond with the 'vault stories' and all of its dark mysterious context, much of this, his father and grandfather shared with him, though there were others who had the stories and strange experiences associated with the mythology.

Lorenzo's companions included his school friend's Carlos, Janice, Brine and Dalgorius and all of them had somewhat the same idea's of finding the 'Holy Grail' as it were in all this, and with this type of philosophy, it only implored them more to search further. Lumina, Lorenzo's sister Lumina remembers telling him about a dream of that spider they may have been searching for in the archaeological finds and she spoke of it many times before and only after she had that dream having described it as such. "It descended from above, always permeated by a light emission behind it, so it was silhouetted; its imposing body shocked me as it was no ordinary spider but seemed to go from spider to humanoid." She felt she needed to tell her brother, especially about it. He was the one who heard this without prejudice and seem to understand her anxiety and at this point in thought, he was startled and he turned around, "What's all this commotion about?", he said. Strange noises that weren't specific were heard in the area that they had been searching in only a day before, for the area that they had initially covered had been one or two kilometres square and was getting closer to the source. The group's over-all distance was fifteen kilometres including the coast where these strange occurrences had been.

The 'tomb of the time vault' is what they began calling this place because of the ceramic tiles, usually found in the older tombs in the area and that the caverns were in the same location they had been searched for in succeeding times for any treasures from past searches. There was a rumour of pirates stashing loot with the exception of the ceramic pottery tiles and shards and old Portuguese and foreign coins, nothing exceptional had been found. About a week into the find with the tiles, a series of energy waves had been felt in a small pocket of ground, causing a tingling sensation on the body of a few of the group, it caused Carlos and Brine these sensations more acutely with Brine stooping over. "I'm now feeling sick", he said. This was to be their discovery, the turning point in the search and later that day Brine, with the advice of his companions, admitted himself to the local medical centre for a check up and it was unknown as to what the cause was, however it would be later that they knew the more mysterious source of the problem.

Deliberately they and Lorenzo had used metal rods to check for irregularities in the ground, they checked the certain rocks and ground in and around the caverns that the sounds seemed to be sourced. They say the crystals in the caverns themselves had this effect but how much Lorenzo took this to be truth, or not, still had him sceptical on the whim and which included old school friend's and looked around various places, finding bits of ceramic from the older civilization close to the area of Kalambaka and once in a while a piece of metal of a unfamiliar construct would turn up and this generated interest, as the metal in general was old generally unmarked coinage. He pondered, "What was the significance of what his father had told him?"

There had been lights in the area and these had mysteriously been appearing in caves from no apparent source of which had been reported before by locals. Delgorius exclaimed on this, and was just as sceptical as the rest of the team but now though, everyone was spooked by the event. "My hairs are on end, there is definitely electricity in the air and in the earth," said Janice. "Where's the source", Brine questioned as he looked around intensely as was the rest of them. Lorenzo felt the source point was what he found in the cleft in front of them, was what looked to be the small cavity entrance to a cave, covered partially by tufts of lush grass. There was a peculiarity in that the cavity was rather uniform in appearance and he thought that it was just meters away, probably eight from where the energy wave was still coming through from and pulling away the grass camouflage, as they approached. There it appeared,

7

the opening but to be too small for an adult to climb through, Janice thought she might have a go at trying to climb through, though somewhat hesitantly. She was seemingly small enough to get through and which with some pushing , she managed. It was however on shining a torch into the cavity, she could pick out some tile inside it and again as she exited the now larger entrance, then dug around again. It seemed to expand it but not by much, she then entered but approached with a cavers helmet equipped with a light and went in with her and her petite floral dress, she was not dressed for caving and squeezing through this opening with the point being the brazen attempt to enter this hole in the ground was that some were amused by the display of boldness and being observed by all except Brine and who was still at the medical centre still being observed and for whatever had done this to cause his condition which included dizziness, had alluded his general medical practitioner, though put it down to tiredness.

After about a minute of quiet study by Janice and a worried group calling out to her, that it was at this point that she started her way back after being able to go no further but on her having come out, she appeared startled. "There are some more tiles almost like a mezzanine inner doorway and there intact!" Lorenzo leaps down to her as if he was going to propose "Intact?", "Yes, Intact, like that of a community hall", saying it matter of fact and he and the group hugged Janice and laughed as he slapped hands with the rest of the group.

That night there was a cause to party although partying was different to a lot of what other people who partied hard were doing. There's was more of a boardroom set up and feel and as if one more piece and the final one at that had been found and now solved. It was Delgorius who had a certain melancholy about him this night. "What's wrong, Del?", as he was sometimes called for short, Lorenzo asked him. "Years ago I speculated about what we might find one day, the vault and what it really could be, I..." he stammered "I know I had this dream about the spider." At his saying this, Lorenzo and Janice gasped. "Why didn't you tell us before! You know you are truly with us in this, his sister had this dream you know?" she said, saying this in a half serious, half jovial way. "No!" Del exclaimed in virtual disbelief. "Yes, my sister did have this dream, a spider descended down upon her, which was her recollection of it." "My God, the same dream for me, with a bright light, that's word for word my friend, word for word." stated Lorenzo. He had a faint smile, "It's obvious where getting a message from here but what?" exclaimed Del. "Yes it's true", said Janice, and Brine had now a quizzical look was there, hearing about his brother Del. "What of this situation?", Lorenzo said to the rest of the group. There was a stagnant hesitation from them, he continued. "What are your thoughts and feelings on this?", it was clear that Brine from the start of the evening was in deep thought, if not perturbed and this was increasing as well as with Carlos, he was another in the group who was clearly so! The uncomfortable silence was then broken. "About something in a last life, I was unable to carry out my wishes on...something?...And...I'm just afraid I might lose this opportunity again.", he pronounced. At that moment a strange sound pronounced itself in the room that they were in and seemingly from the orator of the moment, Carlos. Like a high pitch humming, almost like an insect and the smell of tar and camphor became pronounced. Uneasiness grew in the room, something was wrong with Carlos and he went into unconsciousness, his eyes grew darker and an unearthly feature of light projected itself like a laser beam, beginning to create a red spot on his temple. "We are the Henuburians", this came through his audibly different voice which was much deeper as if his vocal cords had been manipulated, and the rest of the group became faint and went into a kind of stasis. "Today that link that was made aeons ago and will be re-established with you, this small group but only you and Delgorius will know." "Know what?" Del inflected. "That in time will be revealed", Del was transfixed, not entirely believing what he was seeing and feeling. The entity continued, "I am part of the collective of their tribe, the unconscious, we came down aeons ago and left our mark on humanity. Our covenant will, to do, have not yet been completed. They before us did its cycle..Dig out the cave entrance, there you will find the beginning of a labyrinth, follow it to the doors vault, you will know when you see it." At that instant, the buzzing noise stopped and all came to in that moment. Carlos, on coming out of his sleep/stasis, had his hand in his pocket as if to already bring something out of it, a purple crystal. It was as if the group had sensed what had happened, especially when their gaze fixed in on the crystal. It seemed to bring up hidden memories, it was three by one point five centimetres at the width, somewhat ordinary but perfect to look at, it was like a crystal from a chandelier. "I found it right there where the energy wave was, just below the soil line," Carlos inflected. "That's when I started to feel sick, when I saw the crystal in Carlos's hand, that sensation was strange, it made me forget." "Now we know", said Brine. They had been unconscious, everyone agreed to have a similar vision that the crystal projected and it then began to lowly levitate over the table with some sort of thermal flash and then a pervading glow of iridescent purple light filling the entire room, it continued this for about a minute.

Then it emanated a holographic projection of planet Earth but very different. The continents were dryer looking, with some further variance of colouration; it then got closer as if projected by some off-world space-ship/craft. The surface showed lake beds, smatterings of foliage and pockets of forests. There were some buildings that were unfamiliar but of the same colour as the landscape, they included a gothic architectural look with domes, then to a familiar looking coastline, one in fact that they had just been working near. Further deliverance of the message projection showed the ship slowing and to their astonishment, the shape of a doorway appeared in the coastal hillside and then an even deeper audible tone projected then that of Carlos, this vibrated out from the crystal. There was an electrical atmosphere in the room. "This is your territory! The same location you were today." From the hologram projection, the shape of a shadowy circle could be seen being cast by none other than a large saucer shaped craft, it ended with, "Go seek!" The projection then cut out with a sonic shriek and low hum. The light from the crystal dimmed and cut out as it floated back down to the table. Tears were streaming down the face of Janice. Brine and Lorenzo however all stayed relatively calm but emotional. There was concern and worry coming from the host of the deliverance of the message, Carlos.

Chapter 2. The dig

It was Sunday morning, the following day, it was quiet and there was a sense of passivity in the group and they were staying in Lorenzo's house and this had somehow bonded them together, even more, so much now that they had shared about their lives even more and the crystal had become a sacred item to them now tied them all in, this little purple crystal. It was decided that morning to go and excavate the entrance to 'the doorway', as it was now termed by them, this had also become a special shrine in a sense.

What geological equipment they had they took with them was collected quickly, picks, shovels and other geological equipment was now at the ready, there was now only one thing to do and that was to excavate. With this now under way and it was no different to any of their other digs, except for the fact that they knew the answers to the 'Vault' they were undertaking to unearth and the rush of information that came in the night before, which in itself changed their lives in a permanent way and adding to this, the clues the tiles had revealed with the symbol which they had come across earlier. Now the opening was truly revealing something in the light, something truly remarkable! It would have seemed that the interior revealed the inside of a tomb entrance way, a huge expansive labyrinth like interior and the hexagonal shape of what appeared to be an unusual type of construct with three versions of itself one on top of the other, in smaller dimensions and with everything else within this place looked too scientific to be what seemed to be tomb like, add to that, everything was either grey or pearl tones.

"My God, Carlos!" turning to him and then the group, "What have we stumbled upon?!" Janice entreated. "It's our find, the find of the century!" Insisted Delgorius. The room sprawled in to what seemed to be a chamber that stretches into a forever continuous light and areas of darkness and there seemed to be a heavy transmission field in the room as they all began to notice the sound of moving parts that made a bizarre vibration din. Just at this moment, some of the flooring began to descend around the hexagonal object that gradually formed the top of an obelisk and the sound began to vibrate louder from the centre of it and the same peculiar buzzing noise was heard as was the night previous to them, all from the purple crystal but exceptionally more so! Immediately the ground began to rumble in a low tone and something began to lift upward, similar to what had been seen from the outside doorway and a shaft like object slowly ascended from the ground, it was from this similar device where the energy field was felt by Brine and what had been underneath him that day, there was one inside as well. The group ran to investigate the outside but the room had been darkened and now could not leave as there was a force field blocking them!

The rumble had stopped but the buzzing sound much like a computer terminal continued inside the labyrinth, echoing in a strange insect like way that was produced by the places huge expanse. Electrical flashes were prevalent from the obelisk device and a glowing pervaded this hexagonal object and the inside of the entrance, they agreed that this was the 'time vault'! A thunderous bellow echoed through the chamber and in a mono tone voice that had a slight epicurean/gothic accent meaning it was very monotone with a sophisticated articulation in the wording, a statement was made, "Welcome, chosen one's, you found yourself here not by chance, there are no chances you have taken that wouldn't have led you in this direction and eventually all will be revealed to you". Brine was feeling particularly fearful, so too Delgarius, it showed as they all began to panic a little in their particular mannerisms and quirks of personality but as if following the same feeling Lorenzo and Janice calmed them, "It's going to be alright guys", Lorenzo said quietly, the voice continued, "This is the dawning" and stopped abruptly only to hear a strange sound source by an unknown location being piped in throughout the labyrinth, the group looked around at each other but Lorenzo had a slight grin on his face, Carlos and Janice began grinning as well, Brine and Delgarius, didn't know what to do but looked rather serious, the voice then continued, "My friend's tonight you have a choice handed to you then, by none other than the ancient race, called the 'Henuburian's', we are like yourselves as humans, many and varied. Immediately a holographic image appeared and aghast at seeing this, the group looked onward in amazement at the image shown.

Chapter 3. The humanoid

Although the figure appeared humanoid, it definitely was not human, with six additional arms like that of a spider, it was approximately four feet in height. "My image is being projected also into your minds, release your fears friend's because I know all of you well, I met you the other night". The group began to murmur and the being continued, "The chamber is being made available to you". An all pervasive light glowed through the walls of the chamber and doors from the centre of the room began to open, what then appeared was a labyrinth of silvery grey metal with a bluish hue and gold. It felt silken smooth to touch as did most things in the labyrinth.

The obelisk as shown by a transparent section of the chamber facing the entrance to the front appeared to physically close and there was still uneasiness there in the room. "It must be ok, they've made us welcome whomever they are, these Heniburian's and we've search this and ourselves over the past time, it's our destiny", Janice stated.

12

There ahead of them in the chamber were large glass tubes that seem to be metallic at the base like glassy steel where they reached to the ceiling to about twenty feet into a seeming fog, there were also other that were shorter some ten feet. A rhomboid shaped being appeared underneath a waterfall type cascade of water with what looked like a computer console above it and at once the glass tubes raised.

"I haven't met them yet", replied Janice. "Yes, this is all worrisome", Brine concurred in agreement. "Why hasn't it said any...?" Lorenzo was about to finish."These glass tubes are your transport to our world". The image of this being again projected onto the podium in front of them this time, "I am also a representation of the image that has been projected in to your dreams, though some of you have not yet understood this, it is what you are destined to know. This is our offering to you, you are free to choose if you would like to go...to our world, to view it and then come back...that's if you wish to." "It's what I've waited my whole

13

life for!" Carlos shouted out. Brine started toward the crystal tubes transportation, "No!!...Brine...why are you going without me!" Janice shouted and grabbed him, he turned and looked at her, "I'm not leaving you, isn't it obvious? How could I, is there room for two in the transport tubes?" "No, each has single tube to themselves, this is the safest way and they would not work if this was activated, there's safety involved and not that it can't be done but we have a universal protocol to adhere to." "Brother, don't leave me behind!" said Delgorius and was obviously upset with his brother's decision. "Then come with us!" retorted Brine. His brother hesitated."Where are you taking us if I go?" Brine said to the alien being. The alien beings finger pointed to a screened holographic projection and what came into view, astounded them all, it was a beautiful paradise of trees, mountains and cathedral type buildings, towers and pyramids. "My God, it's beautiful", Brine murmured, and they watched for what seemed an eternity, it was a world unlike what they had seen before. "Don't hesitate Del but do as you wish." said Brine. It seemed as if everyone except Lorenzo had made the decision to go, then all eyes from the group fixed on Lorenzo. "Come on, try it!" shouted Delgorius, whilst Brine and Janice beckoned with hand gestures, finally shaking his head at them, he gave a smile. The alien image stood behind him.

Lorenzo, looking at the group one last time, Carlos, Brine, Janice and Delgarius whom was the last one to go as they boarded the tubes, it was then that something between them was going to be imparted that was to be from the inner depths of their spirits. The crystal tube proceeded to close over them simultaneously and the light wave that came through made them appear to disappear in an instant. Lorenzo, stood there motionless for what seemed an eternity, he turned to the Heniburian seemingly on a more familiar basis to the appearance of it but now the image had appeared to be materialised, the idea of being bitten by love or illusion lingered in his mind but it raced. The alien spoke, "You have hungered for this moment, tears streamed down Lorenzo's face, "My friend's...are they...will they...?" The alien finished off his sentence, "Be back?", "Yes Lorenzo, you will be back with them." A bewildering but somehow familiar union of mind seem to take place between them, as though assimilating the information that had been received and he could now hear the words in his mind.

"You will have visions my friend, lots of them, as the alien was saying this, his body seemed to assimilate a more humanoid form, Lorenzo's perceptions were also changing, this

14

made him feel slightly uneasy and with the alien now walking behind him, had added to this. He then felt a wave of euphoria and a strange sensation of homesickness as if he had been away from home along time. The alien now made it clear for him to leave the labyrinth by pointing to the doorway and he proceeded to the upper floor that had been contained by a pneumatic device. He walked toward and out the door to the scene to which they had dug and walked into the hillside and no doorway appeared from outside of this. "This is so you will know who greeted you, your father spoke of the vault, Lorenzo, somewhere in your history we have made a visitation but only you will know what to look for", "What! What am I looking for?" Retorted Lorenzo. "It's in your heart and soul", replied the alien, "Now you must search your mind, only then will it be revealed to you, only then will you know the labyrinth of the vault". A great wave of exuberance swept his psyche. "Yes, I remember something", "Go home then and you will receive the rest of the information, my name is, Ismondera, goodbye for now, Lorenzo." he finished saying.

There had been children watching from a hill top, to see, Lorenzo, talking to what appeared to be a hillside. Giggling, the children went in to further inspection of the hillside. They looked at each other in astonishment of the phenomenon. "I saw him come out of the hillside", said one of the children, Derek said to the other, they continued warily and continued. Lorenzo had just walked out of the hillside after having finished speaking with Ismondera. They kept on approaching the hillside at this point and Lorenzo on walking away had seen them go in. He stood flabbergasted, not believing that Ismondera would leave the door open, however he knew the character of Ismondera and that no harm was intended, he stayed and watched and after a minute they ran out.

Chapter 4. Renee

Renee was Lorenzo's girlfriend and partner for six years and they lived together close to the site that they had been investigating and she was not at all interested of late of going on any field expeditions that were organised by Lorenzo's friends. Lorenzo and Renee, had awoken to the sounds of the chorus of morning birds on a typical morning and on getting up, she called to Lorenzo. "Honey, are you making breakfast?" "Yes love, bacon 'n' eggs with toast",

"Ah good" she said, tying on her morning robe, she went to greet Lorenzo with a kiss. "What time did you get in?", "Late", he said with almost no expression, she then walked in the direction of her craft basket, and fumbled around for her crochet fabric that was popular with her. She turned and was seemingly agitated. "What did you get up to the other night, I can smell wine over you." "Nothing, I was here, Love" "Your digging buddies!" she insisted. On occasion she was come along and meet with the geologist buddies of his and go along with them and though interested enough, Lorenzo had put those things to the back of his mind. His hands steady on the kitchen bench now, he suddenly had an urge to tell Renee and it quickly became the foremost in his mind but realised he could not clarify on the question. "There away somewhere...hmmm. Where exactly?" She mumbled saying it in a mumble just audible for him to hear. "Somewhere exotic, one of the Pacific Islands I guess", he retorted back, feeling at this point half-insane and knowingly that he could have explained this way better. "You know, I always told them, you are crazy for doing this! All of this! And I just told them to do something else for a change and that's what they did", at this point she laughed, "Yeah, you think I believe that!" she said in a half curt and serious way. "Now look, I've worked that farm and not only that, I've worked, looking after it for forty odd years with a father who wouldn't get off my back because of that labyrinth he'd speak of just about day in day out and why I'm a part time archaeologist and it would be good for a change for once that something different could occur and I've had my share of the load! However in light of this something else has cropped up", he said in a more sombre and serious tone. "Yes, well I know! I know...darling, you can't have been this excited and not had something happen but in this you're forgetting our relationship!?" At this she made her way to through the door in to the lounge room as though the conversation was over. He bobbed his head in thought and turned to the lounge room and walked slowly over to the doorway, "Darling, it all happened so quick", apprehensive at first in saying this he proceeded and looking at her in the eye, continued, "Brine found this artefact, a purple crystal" he took in breaths, "In fact it started to do some strange things to us and that was before the visitation type episode, we had it happen here whilst you were out at your mother's." "Lorenzo! What visitation and in this house? How could...?" "Lorenzo began, "No, no it was more like a phenomenon, completely benevolent!" "What did it do to you then!?" "We...we...fell into a trance like state", "How, you're telling me, that purple crystal did that!?" "Yes!" she let out a crying whine, "Now you're scaring me! So go on, out with it, why did this happen!" Her eyes wide..."Well that's what I'm about to bring up. Um, this is going to sound ridiculous...an entity or an extraterrestrial, channelled through us, well Carlos." Renee could not believe her ears, hands up to her face below her eyes. "Oh my God...why does that shock me?" "Because you've seen them before haven't you!" Exclaimed Lorenzo, With Renee being predisposed to this psychic phenomenon beforehand, she knew what had somehow taken place. "I could feel something two days ago, that must have been what happened, right!?" "Yes and I have found this map my father left me, plus something about our family tree!" "What is it?" "I don't know all of it but there is something, Dad has that item, I must find out about it." After some discussion of travel arrangements, Renee, agreed she would accompany, Lorenzo and the next day they set off for Athens where his father lived.

Chapter 5. Bus to Athens

Lorenzo's car was not working and at this point that was the last of his concerns. He set off by bus some three hundred and forty six kilometres to the capital Athens, Renee concerned for Lorenzo, came with him, they caught the late afternoon bus to Athens. It seemed to be along journey and they spent most of their time sleeping their way there, making three stops, a total of four hours. It was at this time that Renee, would try to extend the conversation with him and he was determined not to get into the details as she had the suspicion not all was as it seemed and of which, this feeling grew within her as the trip to Athens ensued and she kept on thinking of this whole thing to do with the town itself. She did not press further him further, thinking things would unfold as they went.

It was early morning dusk and the people of Athens were either getting ready for work or just waking up. There were soft glimpses of light over the horizon with pinks, mauves and purples, dusting the horizon and the city and its old Roman ruins with its splendid light.

People dotted the streets here and there. "Welcome to Athens, hope you enjoyed your journey with us? Voiced the bus driver, with the sign of the bus depot showing similar phrasing, finally then pulling up the bus. "Are you with it, awake?" said Renee in a tone that sounded more melancholy than anything else did. "Yes, yes, I am!" He said as if woken from a slumber of thought, "You just seemed so distant", he took a long look at her. "No Renee, it just seemed like a long trip and besides, I get to see my father for this and probably for the last time."

Chapter 6. Onlio, chance meeting

Lorenzo called up his father and let him know that he would be arriving to Athens within the next twenty four hours. Onlio, his father had lived in his apartment for two years but had owned it for some twenty-seven years after having it on a lease/rent basis and having moved a few times into it.

Meanwhile, his father is in his apartment and has just come back from shopping. "My son..ah Lorenzo, where are you my son, see you soon?", he said to himself quietly. Later the next morning after having breakfast, he then pushed the door forward as he moved into his bedroom which had views of the Athens skyline being on the twentieth floor which gave him great views. In his wardrobe was a small wood box with things from his past, a past he remembered with some disquieting reminders. He recalled in his mind, walking in this brush land area, where fifty years ago, one of them disappeared without a trace", he remembered how distraught their parents were and a tear rolled down his cheek in recollection of the incident. The mother had cancer and the father had disappeared, also after relentless searching and had began taking the top off the box and started to unfold the cloth that hid the crystal not uncommon looking, large, with a dark pearl colouration with a luminosity type lustre to it and that he use to use back on the farm near Kalambaka, in his meditations, it was of a sizable acreage on that farm good for long strolls and getting lost in the past. Carefully he took out the dark crystal shaped rock and closing his eye's, gripped it tightly, it then began to glow a magnesium bright light. "No!" he cried as a flood of memories inundated him. Tears streamed down his face, he got up and started towards the patio slider to get onto the balcony. From the bus, Renee and Lorenzo, had picked up their luggage on going out to the taxi rank, Lorenzo put out his arm for a taxi and started out to the address of his father's apartment, which wasn't far away, "Archarnon street, please." He scanned frantically the skyline and to where his father's building was, closed his eyes and took in a deep breath to face the memories from his past.

Meanwhile, back in the town near Kalambaka, there a resident of the area the archeological group had studied, was alone and studied the a slope of the hill of the area the children had been seen playing some days prior to this. It was there she found the discrepancy that made her question what she had been looking at and she began walking over to it and it was at this point that a light started to emanating from it like a beacon, beckoning her, pulsing or blinking on and off and on approach of it, then disappeared again.

They made their way to the apartment on the twentieth floor and finally made their way to the door which was already open and inside was his father, "Dad"!, he stretched out his arms and both gave hugs one to the other, I thought you'd have gotten here earlier, "No, well you know how it can be Dad, we got here by bus, car's not working right", replied Lorenzo. His father had a rock and crystal display and Renee had noticed this, taking particular interest in it and walked over to it, "Wow, this is a great crystal display", his father had poured coffee's and was about to serve out, when he put his coffee on the bench and decided to go to the wood box in his bedroom and pulled out that crystal, he brought it out, "here's one I've found and in that area Lorenzo, where we did all that digging, look at it", said Onlio, as he bobbed it up and down in his hand and you can have that." Handing it to either one of them, so first Renee held it, then Lorenzo, no Dad, it's yours", "No, I insist, take it" as his father put it in Lorenzo's shirt pocket and patting it. "Ok, thanks for that Dad." His father gave him a quizzical look, "I want you to know, I've held that crystal for years and I now want you to look after it, it's from the Vault area." "You mean the cave we found the other day, Dad?" "There's lots of caves son", "Not this one, Pop?" Renee walked in almost tearful and went to hug Lorenzo" Onlio, chuckled, "You really did…" Bellowing a chuckle at this point. "You kids probably need some rest from this. "I'm worried about him, Onlio", cried Renee. "No, don't be, your blessed, the both of you!" Now go out you two, I now know why I gave you this crystal, son, because it has brought me some grief, I know it will help now!" "Our friends went with them", said Lorenzo, almost in disbelief. "Does anyone else know?", said Onlio in a rather serious overtone. "No Dad, just us", Lorenzo replied back. "Don't worry they will be back!", Onlio imparted to them as though this stuff can just happen. "I know these beings, they have been in my dreams too", she imparted back to Onlio. "Ok Renee", he replied back,

19

she hugged Lorenzo's father. "If there is anything I can do to help you, I will, the both of you. Forget about your experiences for now, go out, look around, have something to eat." replied Onlio.

They then went out and had a meal at a BYO restaurant and caught up on old times and they had a wonderful day, they spent another day in Athens and then decided to go back to Kalambaka, not before Renee, was wanting to stop at her Grandmother's. For now there was a psychic experience that began to unfold as at the point that it had begun to unfold in a sub-conscious way, unbeknownst to Onlio and that this would happen from the apartment balcony that had been nerve wracking enough for Onlio but definitely there were more answers than some questions for Lorenzo and it was as if a heavier weight had been set down on them again.

On their way to the bus terminal as Lorenzo and Renee chatted on the sights and sounds of Athens, the crystal in his pocket began to pulsate light and became hot if anything. This was spotted by a some passer bys, at this point Lorenzo pulled it out of his pocket and noticed a ringing in his ears but more notably that most of the people around him were holding their hands over their ears. "Your alarms going off, Sir", said one man "Is it, what the..?" Lorenzo took a look and was astonished and shocked by this as he looked at it and now he looked at the policeman on his approach to him and awkwardly looked at Renee and a few of the passer bys. Renee was astounded and in almost disbelief as well, it stopped abruptly, the police man asked for some identification off, Lorenzo, a definite change was in the pipeline, as now he gave his father a call to tell him what was occurring.

Asking his father what should be done, his father replied, "It will be alright, you'll see son, you'll see.", "Renee, was concerned and Lorenzo was upset by this but intrigued, he thought nothing of it as he then tried to pack it in his bag but was apprehended and ask to relinquish the item as it was deemed dangerous and they made off to the bus depot and for Lorenzo, he had the crystal and now the memory of his father and the love of Renee it was all that mattered to him, it would seem that not only was that the focus of attention but a group of police made their way to the location they had been standing when they had been approached by the police officer and looking back where the policeman had first apprehended Lorenzo, he and Renee were feeling entrapped.

20

He now possessed the crystal, that after all those years was in his father's possession and that had locked into more questions about his father and himself than answers. "It is a doorway to the other world", his father once said, also saying, "This stone will open up the Labyrinth, as he remembered him saying", he muted the noise from his mind and focused around his thoughts on this matter, "But wasn't that the Labyrinth I found back at Kalambaka, is there yet another?" he thought. "Alright, it's time to go, hurry!" shouting to Renee, hurriedly grabbing her hand. "Go? Why are you running? They are going to want to ask you questions, Lorenzo! If this is why, they were after the crystal?" she said, "You don't understand because now I've remembered, this will open it", he brought out his father's dark crystal. "This will open the Labyrinth back home!" and she paused, now looking concerned, "C'mon!" Grabbing her arm he started to run, she dislodged it with a twist and paused, "Why Lorenzo, it's just an ancient burial ground!" He laughed "No this is no grave, this holds the secrets to time and space, an alien hall of records." Her eyes fixed on him and then the crystal, "You mean the place you've been telling me about is this?" she said "Yes, your psychic, you should see what this is! How many times have I told you to believe in you and your gift", "Oh my God, now I know what you're telling me, we have to guard this crystal", she said. "Yes that's what I've been trying to tell you in a roundabout way", rolling his eyes as he said this. She didn't need to be motioned along, Renee knew exactly what to do next, they were anatomic, almost robotic, they felt like they weren't in control of the moments that followed.

Chapter 7. Lorenzo's anguish

The alien stood at the threshold of an over-view of a compartment of many rooms that seem to stretch for miles, looking like an underground base, this was by no means so and on them stood glass compartments to what was thousands of people.

To the woman who approached the hillside, the alien now looked, "In history, many have gone missing and never come back from history, saved by some event", the woman smiled as the alien said this, he continued..."You will have to be put in stasis until certain things happen 'sister being.'" She sat in a chair overlooking the huge compartmental labyrinth. The alien finished off by saying, "Behold, they will be alive in a transformed state as I transform." A light from one of the crystal tubes seem to disperse into the alien as every other single tube in the labyrinth seem to light up. The portal tube closed over her, two or more on the floor remained behind her. The being had now a more humanoid appearance." I now await Lorenzo and Renee, their destiny is closer."

He made his way back to the abyss in his mind, spirit and soul as he gripped Renee's hand tightly with the crystal stashed in his pocket. "I will prevail with this, I am determined, I will not fail", he thought devoutly in his mind with the tone of apprehension thronged by a deeper tone of boldness. He had given this a whisper with a slightly nervous inflection in his voice at times. His way back home was by catching the bus, the only option and after purchasing the ticket and waited in a line to be boarded. It was at this time that Onlio, called an ambulance, he was having fluctuations in his breathing. All this had been very heavy for him.

A few of the police were seen along the way but did not seem to react, although Lorenzo's nervousness was about the dark crystal's apparent ability to cause change in others and it amplified his thoughts and images relative to the crystal itself. "It does not seem to have any apparent effect over me!" he said, turning to Renee. "It's got to do with something I..." he paused "We've got to fulfil!", "I do not know any longer if I want this, I will have to leave you! Just go Lorenzo!" she shouted, sobbing and continued. "Fulfil what you had to do in your destiny." she cried. At this point heads were turning in the bus. "But I want you with me!" Lorenzo didn't want to see it any other way. "No! It has some sort of power over you, you are linked to it!" Sobbing as she held her face. "I've dreamt this alright!" he said. "No, I'm leaving you, I must go!" she retorted. Folding her arms at the bus depot, he pleaded with her, "Come with me, we will sort it out together" "No, just go!" she again shouted, he became bemused and upset "but..." he paused "Your right Renee, I can't go on like this, it's stayed with me my whole life and I can't deny it, with or without you, I have to go on...it won't go until I face it!" She looked at him, then held his hand, "I just can't take it anymore, I love you but I can't go with you!", and let go of his hand abruptly. He proceeded to step onto the bus and felt the procession of the next phase of his journey was about to take place. Tears began to well up in his eyes as he parted ways, looking out to her from the bus both with tears in their eyes, knowing that something was keeping them apart. She kept a look out and later she decided to take another bus.

On the bus back, Renee had decided to make a detour to a relative she had not seen in a while, her Grandmother's house and as now, Lorenzo was her former partner as she saw it and far too traumatized to solve any differences between themselves. Her Grandmother lived on the outskirts of a township called Areopoli, some fifty kilometres away where she lived with Lorenzo and in the meantime there was the fear within Lorenzo, as he did not feel right about what he was going to go into and would have forfeited with his idea and let things go back to the way they were but this was not particularly an option for him and had gone on and off for some time, he was a man truly torn in his mind and knew he would not allow himself to breach the decision on what he would do with the 'crystal' and couldn't.

He slept, exhausted from his trip to Athens, that as short lived as it was, it seem to go on for an eternity, he was sold on that. Ismondera had told him, mind body and soul, literally he would to give his all or nothing. His dream contained the last vestiges of information that he would have to hold onto himself, what he felt was left of it. There was still a longing within him though, that was not entirely clear to him, the formula for success was to let go of it and get on with it. Lorenzo later tried phoning his father but to no avail, no answer. In his memory came that afternoon of his father, was, "Son", he remembers his father saying as he called him most of the time, at a table, he appeared to pull out a black board and some chess pieces to set onto it. "See these chess figures, well, the porn is me and you and let's say this bishop is the rest of society because family is all important". He then used the king and queen because they have more moves and more diversity on the chess board. "Looks inundating doesn't it, as a board game goes and may seem it but with this crystal from the 'time vault' and for what it has planned for you to do will cause more moves for you, this as for the porn", saying this with a grin, he continued, "but it's one move in this that will use your mind, body and soul my son, don't stuff it up!" My Lorenzo, I want to know if this is what you'll do, for me?", "What Dad?" He then took out a vial of dark looking liquid. "What is this Dad?", "It's blood, this is something I know will benefit you, son, and with your permission, with this I give to you", and with his permission Lorenzo accepted based on his belief of what his father had told him and placing a small amount of this liquid onto his own thumb, took Lorenzo's hand and press his thumb onto his son's thumb conjoining their beliefs in that moment, creating a legacy of that story. "You will I know, know what to do with this crystal my boy!" Tears welled up from the emotion of that moment for Lorenzo and ran down his face. His father grabbed his shoulder to show his compassion and encouragement to him. The dark crystal shone at him, Lorenzo looked in amazement. "They gave me this and blessing after blessing has come to our crops, our finances and olive's aplenty my son! They are looking after us Lorenzo." "Who Dad, who?" asked Lorenzo from his tear laden face, looking for assurance from his father. His father smiled under his moustache. Later and secretly, his father cried.

Chapter 8. Renee and Marcie

Renee had made it to her Grandmother's house, she was the only living relative as far as she knew. Her mother had passed away in Cologne, Germany during her travels and remembered going to her funeral several years ago. On approach of the house, which had a Spanish Armada and French provincial appearance, with one garden showing it was full of azaleas and poppies. Renee was uncertain at first as she came to the front porch on approach if this garden was her Grandmother's, Marcie. On seeing her granddaughter, she cried, "Renee, my lovely granddaughter, I've missed you!" and Renee held out her arms as she reciprocated in kind with her, kissing each other on both cheeks as the French do and then Marcie finally rested her head on her, then held her tightly, crying still. "I've missed you my grand-daughter!" "I know grandma! I know." "Now I must tell you about this dream I had, now stay for tea, I'll make us a snack, we have a long day my beautiful."

Some time passed as they made small talk, she poured out water with rose and lime mixture and then led Renee down one side of the patio, close to a reading room that was that was a lavishly furnished living area with much character. They decided to go to the township and catch up on shopping and friends, old friend's some new and some old for Renee but had a great time, especially the special Greek feta and coffee of the region. Marcie and Renee came back to the living area and began resting into their chairs, chatting, catching up on gossip, movies and the family tree, finally Marcie quietened, "I had an awfully strange dream, it seemed to be this spider...person, I had this dream before!" her daughter looked at her intensely. "Grandma, we've been through this before and you know I've had this too, so you're not alone" and stretched out her hand from the chair she rested on to her

24

grandmother's shoulder and Marcie grasp her hand in response, both her and her grandmother had, had this talk many years before and at different intervals in time as this phenomenon had effected them too in many ways. She continued, "This time it came to take you away", she said raising her walking stick. "What does it mean...why?" Renee said, her voice pertinent. "Grandmother, what is you see?" she whispered, "Like a grown adult but also like an expectant child, I see you different", Marcie replied. "I have seen too, Grandma", she whispered as she was used to calling her as a little girl. Her Grandmother smiled, looked at her and caressed her cheek, wiping a tear. Tears again began to well up in her eyes as she spoke this passionately, "You are not alone my child, we are not, they are our guardians and have been for quite some time". They were getting to know each other from different, now more perspectives and in a lot more comprehensive ways, they talked for hours on end, recounting their history and time together.

Chapter 9. Lorenzo's disparage

"Just a little closer", he cried tearfully and dropping to his knees in the long grass, a strange sensation swept him as if the impossible had just occurred and happened to him, a sensation that made him turn around and rush to the telephone as if his mobile had been playing up. Lorenzo was going to call Renee's mobile but got no response. "Hers must be playing up, where is she!", he thought in concern and panic and then thought of the children that had gone to the hillside near Kalambaka and decided that what was wrong was about to take place to Onlio, a miracle for his father, he had that feeling. He thought that then there was inquiries as to an official paranormal investigation, took place even in light of the events that had been?

A combination of optimism and dread filled Lorenzo, as he looked at the three inch long dark crystal, he noticed the hexagonal shape, that of quartz and yet its texture, size and weight spoke of something quite different to that and besides the sound that it had made, it could produce heat as well and being too close to it over a period could produce a strange nausea. He felt compelled to further listen to the messages even though he had instances of wanting to smash it, though the feeling was diminishing.

The vision quest now as Lorenzo could see it was almost over, "How was he to maintain what the crystals power was doing to him?", he would think, it made him feel dread and yet it redeemed him and he took this time getting to the steps at looking at the crystal, super-imposed against the village landscape and sky as though it had the power to flatten both land and sky and his concern was turning to despairing. "What are my friend's doing?" he thought as he went back inside the farm house, closing the door partially, when then there was a knock at the door, breaking his thought, he went to answer it, "Hello, where have you been Lorenzo!?" It was his good neighbour and friend, Tom. "I've got some of last year's crops oil and pulled out some of the bottled olive oil, then sucked a finger as if he had tried some, "Bread?" as if to say to Lorenzo for him to be invited in, "Come in, Tom", he said to Lorenzo then that is what Lorenzo did, "Yes, I'll get some", he said reassuringly but grabbing some out of the refrigerator. It was one of their favourite past-times, to eat their own bread with their own olive oil. "Mmm yum, this is good, Lorenzo try some!" He seemed to be in a self-imposed stupor from the wine after about five minutes. For once in his life, the accent of a childhood friend and neighbour, with smooth olive oil and crusty Greek bread did not help him take notice, he was in a daze looking to the hearth, as if it was a shrine, staring motionless at nothing. "Shit Lorenzo! c'mon...what's wrong?" Lorenzo stroked his chin" "I...I", he murmured "My girlfriend left me" he said tearfully and paused for a while whilst his hand stroked both his mouth and chin. Saddened by this his neighbour retorted, "I'm sorry for your loss...Lorenzo my friend, you won't be getting back together again?" Looking starkly and tearfully at Tom and with the event that went on during the day, he then went into deep thought and cried into his hands. Tom cautiously thought about what to say next but took it as cue to say something immediately, "You don't know what happened Lorenzo?", he questioned, "Yes!, No! I don't know", said Lorenzo. "Will you be alright", he continued, "I think so", he said. "Sigh, it will be alright Lorenzo", said Tom as he got up and gave him a shoulder hug with his hand. "You can come over any time, Lorenzo", he then parted and left the door ajar. Lorenzo stopped in his tracks and looked around at the ambiance of the place and having not ventured downstairs to investigate the cellar, decided that this is what he would do.

Chapter 10. Renee and Marcie's goodbye

The parting was a difficult one with her Grandmother's weekend stay. Renee had to leave as she saw no other way in coming to terms with Lorenzo. "Do what you have to do but has been to problematic." said Marcie, "Yes, I've loved him so much", with that said, she hugged her Grandmother, "I have to go now Grandma", they were both crying. "I pray for you and me!" Marcie yelled, "I know you will, I'll be doing the same and went to the bus stop and back to Lorenzo.

Chapter 11. Renee and Lorenzo

A dim light lit the far side of the Lorenzo farm house, Renee approached the door with caution and her boyfriend's behaviour had been what she thought to have become, now increasingly irregular, earlier that day. Knocking cautiously, the door opened and there standing with an almost astounded look on his face, was Lorenzo, now speaking monotonically. "Come in my darling would you like a cup of something to drink," now walking over to the kitchen bench, "Tea, cola or something?" He did this in a nonchalant manner as if to cover for the happenings that took place earlier and with a grin on her face, her spirits were up but still a feeling of awkwardness pervaded her. "I'll have tea." she said in a submitting but tensioned tone. "Ok, a tea it is..." he paused and turning to her, "It's good to see you again and how was your Aunt's?", "It wasn't my Aunt's, my...!", she stumbled over her words. "My...my Grandmother", a tear began to roll down her face. He interceded, "She's alright and you my darling, what about you, or is it all of something else?" she paused, "She's alright...see this is what I'm talking about, your line of questioning, is 'fucked up!'","Almost immediately he dropped this assuming position "I'm sorry, I didn't know how you felt, and just...well, everything is not the best at the moment", he said this as if detaching from the seriousness of why she came back. "Hey look, I've got something to show you." Her cup of tea had not been drunk yet and she had been up half hesitating to take the tea or run but followed Lorenzo, up and out of the chair. He motioned down the steps to her and she'd seen

27

these steps time and time again but this time took on a precarious with an uneasiness that swept through her and leading her to the cellar, this brought her to embarking down there by his side. "You'll not believe this, just a few more steps! ha ha, you don't want to be drunk", saying it in a casual and slack manner then added, "Why yes dear, wouldn't you be with what I've discovered!", to this Renee seemed intrigued and her amusement grew. Behind the door emanated a soft glowing light that shone through below the door. Renee was beginning to get suspicious and seized up. On opening this door, Lorenzo's grin turned to an all knowing look on his face as if he had seen something...not belonging to this world. Indeed on it opening, Renee's features changed as if in shock and wonderment.

Chapter 12. Searching

Back at Athens police headquarters, an all point's check had been placed in reference to facial features from that of the policeman's identification check, that of Renee and Lorenzo in what the inspector and the others officer's remembered or now had record of them. Inspector Manos, was in charge of this case and had the investigator's track every bit of evidence and seemingly they had some mysterious leads and tip offs even they considered to be out of the ordinary to what they were used to as being strange, getting Lorenzo's and Renee's matching identity photo's with them as suspects had all been discussed, however they wanted to get to them for questioning as soon as possible.

Their searched carried them to the village near Kalambaka where they lived and it was now early being one am in the morning, and Manos, turned up with other police in another three squad cars comprising of unit office's, special and senior investigators, this was now considered a very big case and in their sight's they had a lead building and up to this moment, they knew with all the information tip offs about the anomalous activities and how they led to the disappearances in the area but was just the tip of the ice-berg.

Almost as anomalous to them but seemingly to carry the influence of high ranking authority, not specifically named but linked to investigations carried out by the police and had a number of their own leads linked into it. The valley around Kalambaka approximately

28

five kilometres away, was where this housing estate was located, having some of the best crops and yield's of olive oil particularly in that region, with an astounding array of oils that carried with it, some of the most remedial therapies used and along with the olive extract was the leaf itself.

Crop after crop of these was apparent now as the officer's and investigator's closed in on Lorenzo. Lorenzo's familiar garden was now the look of a posse of investigator's and Manos, appeared to genteelly knock on the door, he did this lightly as their appeared to be a light on, as if this was to work up to something else, the inspector now thumped on the door hard, "Lorenzo, Lorenzo Archarnon, this is inspector Manos, Athens police, you have nowhere to go...!" Just then from out of no-where and to the surprise of the investigator's, a man flashing his Interpol related credentials followed by two other neatly dressed jacketed men stood by as he stormed over knocking down the wood panelled door as if in disapproval and flexing his authority over the Athens inspector. "Shit!" shouted Manos, and followed him in.

All but a lit white candle had been flickering in the room, casting eerie and strange shadows. "Careful, careful", said one of the now more authoritarian security agents, briskly the house was searched for occupants and as this progressed, it was from out of seemingly nowhere that another group of agents wearing black coloured cover-all's and protective visors appeared. The inspector again was surprised, there was a seeming stand-off with Manos and his investigators, until the credentials were flashed in front of the inspector, and the pressure was on. "Manos, was about to speak but was interrupted, "It seems that our branch has a new name, "Fucking surprises!", said Agent Fasculus. A few chuckles went out. "We are a division of Interpol, I'm team leader Captain Rogius", saying this with a grin and lit up a Bolivian cigar, the agent grinned back, leaving the inspector right out of it but amused. "I'm Inspector Manos, Athens police, shaking both Agents Fasculus and Rogius's hands, raising an eyebrow, "Now, maybe your clearance renders me unable in this case but I have leads that you may not after twenty-four hours, so..." "Inspector, you may stay for now but you'll have to give me feedback for when this case started for you", said Captain Rogius. "About twenty-four hours ago", "Good that's all the information we need for now, Inspector, we can take it from here", "Do you want to hear about the body that disappeared?" said Manos, "You had a body disappear, when and how?" he replied back. "In our morgue, almost sixteen hours ago, in a blaze of light, gone, the body of Lorenzo Archanon's, father, we went into question him

29

but was deceased when we got there, reports say heart-attack", "There's been a lot of paranormal activity around here, we'll stay on top of this." At the go ahead of the security agent, Fasculus, who then gave a nod to both men, they began cordoning off the area to the house, everything had now been established for the security division team to search for Lorenzo.

Chapter 13. The find

It was an hour before the police agents from Athens as well as agents of Interpol had arrived, an apparent steel structure of a door was realized and opened with no apparent obstruction, all the members who were present could not believe what the scope of the place was, once in, they began to walk forward.

Lorenzo, had been finding his way around the labyrinth where there was a metallic look every where he looked with a sulphurous smell. "My father was right all along, he showed me this place, it has no particular grounding in time and space and yet he entrusted me with this knowledge of it!" Renee looked around in suspicion and wonder. It sparkled like an underground and majestic labyrinth should, something you would expect to find with a host of wizards. Checking his compass, he could see that its general direction had to have been where they found the entrance at the hill only three days before. "He kept me in the dark about this, protecting it as though with his life because he did not want another failed crop, this house was his life too...for a century and a half." At this point Renee fainted. Lorenzo was just beyond the doorway where the Agents of Interpol were, they wanted, the who, what and where of this, wanting the bigger picture. Lorenzo now helped his girlfriend over any obstacles and made sure she was secure as he made his way down the labyrinth corridors. Everywhere was a silvery textured metal, yet it glimmered more than any metal that he had seen. Finally the corridors came to a dead end and at this point he remembered something, it looked like a palm scanner of some type, very advanced. He remembered what his father had said about this getting him to the room of Ismondera, remembering now with flashbacks as vivid as if it were yesterday and that he had already been there. Now, Renee was beginning to return to consciousness. He gasped, "It was almost yesterday when he said this..."Ah

Ismondera!", he said loudly, hoping the alien heard, now he knew. He shuddered, an almost apparent fear had swept him. He recoiled also on realizing the artefacts presented in this place were completely strange and different but was now outweighed by then, the fact he felt the aliens presence, "Was it a test?" he thought. Now it was back in his mind as he had seen the extraterrestrial only three days ago. Lorenzo looked around and felt that in fervent fear, that if he acted quickly, he might be able to leave this world behind him. He thought about the wisdom and the love the alien projected toward him and immediately it was clear to him, not to turn back and in fact would serve no purpose as he saw it. Slowly his hand approach the print scanner and static waves began to pulsate and charge slowly and then intensified to the point the vibration caused the walls to vibrate around him and to look dimmer. Suddenly a feeling as if being lifted off the floor and pushed, he instantly found himself back in that familiar surrounding some three or four days earlier, however, this time it was different, looking out at what could only be Ismondera's territory or domain, it was on-board a space-ship/craft. There he saw them, "Crystal tubes, oh my God", he said to himself as he had come to know them, were directly in front of eye's, Ismondera pointed to Lorenzo's cheek, reminding him he could see his tear and then he put his hand on his shoulder as if to say to him, your accepted like family. Renee hugged Lorenzo, "It will be alright." They walked into the tube and an all immersing beam of light filled within it, Lorenzo looked on as Ismondera smiled at them and left off. What seemed as a blinding flash then began to cascade through their entire bodies, facing now toward a light like a magnetic beam, causing them to look fully at it. All manner of things became apparent to them and of their childhood and adulthood combined to a central focus as if everything that was on planet Earth was lifting off or not with him in a permanent way, in his heart of hearts he knew this. A vibration was now becoming apparent to him in his entire body and the light seemed to cascade down, this became space, then deep space.

S8 team was now heading down the corridors of the labyrinth. Tom, was the last witness to Lorenzo's condition, they cross-questioned his affiliation with him, questioning him for any and all the answers to their relationship as neighbours but was now becoming the least of their concerns and a further tip-off had led them to know the possible whereabouts of Lorenzo and Renee, also the security placed a surveillance van at the outside of their premises, certain locations near the village and surrounding area. A secret had been kept by

31

certain members in the S8 team and this lead to knowledge that they had but would not reveal. It took some time but the gate to Ismondera's address had been accessed and it was a matter of minutes before part of the contingency of the S8 team had tried to accessed it, what they saw was a cave with a mezzanine entrance and nothing more.

Chapter 14. Journey to Neru

In the case of deep space, there was no further prevalence to this. It would seem that a floating sensation was enacted upon them, as if by liquid that was velvety smooth, it seemed to be that is was a type of inner perspective, a self-realization of letting go but it began to rip into him just as a feeling of blissful timelessness began to seep in. Lorenzo knew that Renee, was going through the same thing that he was, first a vibration that could be felt, it inked out the light, splitting in all directions, the vibrations increased to a promenade of light sequences that now breach the inky blackness of space that subtly coincided with the rest of the stars and nebula's entering the light, they flew and melded into it, becoming one. It was as if the light had lasted an eternity, then silence. Renee and Lorenzo had felt to seemingly last an eternity, and then it was silence. They had awoken in yet another labyrinth, it glistened like a jewel and everything was seemingly perfect. If the Earth bound labyrinth was anything to go on, then this was by far more, incredible and after departing from the crystal tube, a low humming sound permeated the area they were in. A strange stage assembly was under him, almost as if it was translucent, the more he looked the more he could see there was an underground under the surface. There was a humanoid accompaniment, that was now present around him, with similar characteristics in the face as himself, "Is this my soul group?" he thought to himself and realized he could not distinguish reality as he once did, he felt for the first time that he was really feeling at ease with all around him, his surroundings were strange and beautiful, producing a sense of euphoria, it was clear that this could be his home. "But permanently?" he thought. He wondered if there was another realm like it, he felt it was trying to emulate something to him, his mind and sub-conscious, even to the point that was real and within him even though it seemed completely alien and yet so familiar. "It sure felt and looks genuine, this is not a dream", he thought. The question in his mind was, "Where were Ismondera and the other people?" he had seen.

Lorenzo and Renee walked hand in hand through this Labyrinth that seemed strangely different to the last one. "Can I find the teleporting again?" he thought, he felt again at ease, "It's a transport ship", said the being who seemingly appeared from no-where and looked to be a hybrid human and looked similar to Ismondera, having said this telepathically, both of them reeled back a little. "My name is Recima, and I will be your guide." Renee rested her head on Lorenzo's shoulder in relief, "How could I have doubted you." she said.

Chapter 15. Vested interests

Meanwhile the S8 team had associates who were beneficiaries linked to finances and management and had some corporate based structures involved around their project and they had raised the bar to a certain level and this, what they believed they had to maintain and the cost alone for its attempts so-far reasoned to the company directorate was mainly of a mysterious extraction, that this was the way they had to claim back any if not all they had spent and more through technological advancement and engineered most of it, although the financial factor would be another major challenge for them to overcome. Certain things had not been accounted for because of serving their interests for the most part, almost as if a miniature war was taking place, they would use takeover tactics and there were certain people not sharing in the vast purposes of procuring spiritual fulfilment but to the detriment of it and they would squeeze those genuine others out akin to the vortex of space for greed.

Two special and highest rank of informed of the of S8 team members, were within the division set away to the first labyrinth that, Lorenzo and Renee had been before teleporting out and was a ground base to Ismondera. They knew and had the key to getting to the ship-port that Lorenzo and Renee, had accessed, that being the same teleportation device that, Lorenzo had gone through to get to the ship. Captain Dennis, as he was known when he was a recruit for the tactical security unit, he had served in many security issued hot spots in the world, the second in charge was a Commander Fielding and he too had the same robust portfolio and had trained with psychic remote sensing, part of his history. There was a period in time when he learnt this and passed on information routinely to certain unnamed facilities.

33

Lorenzo had been monitored previously prior to his discovery with his friend's activities, what prompted this was the location and the tip-offs from the extraterrestrial source, the location to the labyrinth that the S8 security division and others like it had knowledge on what possibly they suspected through the mysterious others on the board and the connection that was had, was indirectly related to, Lorenzo. Lorenzo now had this knowledge of what these military people had on file concerning the labyrinth, it was possible that it was a catch twenty-two, the whole idea centred on concealing what was going on in the area.

Lorenzo's father knew a part of the branch that had been involved with the S8 team and for Lorenzo and they had monitored him, rather than his childhood and more on and off, of more recent events. The scenario that was planned was to retrieve anything possible that would keep vested interests, profitable and for this it would be a time of testing for one man in the team, so it was at this moment that a sudden purge of urgency crept upon him, an urgency soon to test his limits.

Chapter 16. Inquiry

It was 9pm and Dennis and Fielding, making tracks at this time and were familiar with the operations of the site and they planned to key in at the teleport tube, each man carrying a cyanide tablet just in case the scenario went bad. Their run was for the vested interests that led them there and they did not have all the facts at large, seemingly the shoe was placed firmly on the other foot including the pants, idea's for advancement.

Captain Dennis, was patriotic to the point of believing the companies decision, ultimately. As if the invite had been set, so that the machine powered up and the ratio of this happening was a factorization that the company implemented with certain procedures surrounding the handling of this case. "The technology will surely start up with the odds of someone to meet you on the other side, it may also want to study you, be it alien or otherwise", he mentioned. The odds of this happening seemed highly remote but the place was peculiar. It was Fielding who set off the hand print device, set amongst tuning forks, it was ready for him and Dennis to leave, they had a sense of fear and euphoria as the beacon of light began to pulse and encase their bodies, the electromagnetic charge left them more in a state of stasis then had Lorenzo and Renee, when travelling with this device. They were now travelling into the other dimension of hyper-space, at this point. Dennis had realized that this was an opportunity for him as he had seen and now to the lengths that, Fielding, had taken and all the training he had done had not prepared him though, for this moment as he was sent back and as he disappeared before his eyes in a burst of white light. Dennis then tried again and was knocked to the ground and he felt a sense of let down, it was at this he realized the tuning forks had compromised his position. He began leaving in a quasi-mortified state and realized that static charge was building in the forks, a defence mechanism? He took off from a now hostile environment, now thundering with heavy bursts of static build up, was this a warning physically from them, had they consciously done this from deep space, light years from anything else? He realized explosions were being set off, electromagnetic pulses along with ensuing fire now began choking the hallways of the labyrinth. Thinking his time was up and that this would be his tomb, he quickly dove out of the entrance from where he came through before. Looking back at the labyrinth, he realized that nothing, no fire and no sound re-emanated from there, in fact when he went back in after the apparent blast, none of the artefacts in there had been affected except for a few scorch marks. This was a technology he could not of imagined and at that moment, staggering, he passed out and went into coma just outside on the hillside, the hologram covered the entrance as nothing of this place was visible. The team from S8 began entering the area and found the comatose, Captain Dennis, lying somewhat blissfully on the ground, Cabort, a head member shouted to him, "Dennis, Dennis!", moving and shaking his body as he tried to awaken him but to no avail, this was a shock to the group, thinking he could handle this mission but immediately sent out members to investigate his tracks until he came to. They came back and there appeared not to be any entrance way available, nothing appeared on their scanning equipment as yet, they quickly rushed him in for further observations.

Chapter 17. Awakened

Fielding awoke in a lit chamber that had an orange glow and that seem to be all around him and a voice rang out in his head being spoken telepathically, "Callum!" This got his attention fully as this had been his childhood name before he underwent an induced identity change through a mysterious organization and had been an orphan at the time his induction began. "Awaken your childhood, Callum!", "No! God damn it! Who is this! Why are you doing thi...this?" he gargled in and struggled in his straight jacket composure and yet he was clad with what was a white skin tight suit in what looked like a hospital with cascading chandelier type lights. He wanted to get his hands on whatever or whoever had said this, "No Callum! Remember who you are instead."

Some time passed as he slipped into a comatose state. "Who are you?" he finally said. "We are the keeper of the vaults, the labyrinth, the one you've just been in, is ours", said the deep and hollow voice. "Ok", said Callum, now calmer and the suit of light surrounding him eased off and he stood up and felt more a sense of peace but tried focusing his attention toward the voice, almost a feeling of being lulled into a trance. "We don't make mistakes, you have not discovered life, real life that is without struggle and whilst that's part of the blessing it's also part of the curse, it comes down to choice. What do you now choose, Callum Field? To work for a company with man-made trials and errors and whom you follow in a monotonous nature? Or a life far improved to the one you have in flux awaiting you?", "What are you offering?" he thought in his mind... At that instant, the room took on the proportions of a three-hundred and sixty degree, holographic projection. This was the same picture projection footage shown to Lorenzo and the group, something of a tourism file of the crystal city and of their planet. Immediately, Callum Field, fell to his knees. "If this is paradise, what is it, that I must do to get there?!" "Just believe and you will go!" That instant a light precipitated projected from the ceiling of the room he was in, where Lorenzo and Renee had come by the same means. Through the light and out to the other side, there he was greeted with a smile from a being with whom he had spoken and recognized his voice. "Hello Callum", he felt a great sense of life force surge through him as if assimilating with the environment he was in. The being placed his hand on his shoulder. "I am, Ismondera we have waited for you for quite some time.", "Me?" he said to himself quietly. "I and the species we are is Henuburian and as guardian's, we place an interest in our inhabitant's, you see, the completion of our people as a work with the addition of you and others is our main focus, to evolve and take joy in our work." Then casting a glance that was piercing from the alien, "With you, your species is what's necessary for our continuance." A question mark hung in Callum's mind and persisted as he was shown the great halls and rooms of the ship. Gilding, artistically done of an exquisite nature but of a strange mausoleum type with balustrade along its stairs and walls in grand fashion, it was impressive to him but seemed very alien at the same time. "Do you have any questions, Callum?" "Yes, yes, just one." "What, why are you coming back?" "He realized Ismondera was not interested in the question", Callum walked on beside him. "You see, our intentions are quite valiant, the company you worked for should be considered the past." Almost dumbfounded, Callum realized a sense of all. He smiled, "how do you know so much about us?" "We've been monitoring your planet for several thousand years and time speeds up." he said in a factual undertone.

Chapter 18. Recollection

The feeling of uncertainty had all suddenly crept into Lorenzo's mind, it always did when he felt something was wrong or a miss and it was like a presence. An example of this, the night his father who was maritally separated had someone over for this particular day, a mysterious woman by the name of Lisa. He was enamoured by her beauty and a concern he noticed in his father as if every law officer had come into town for him, because of her, this made him look uneasy because each time she would come over for a period of about a month, this would set this off in him. Odd things began to happen to his father as well as the olive plantations would have some problems, this led him to work more, downstairs and into the hidden cellar that housed the labyrinth that was more to do with the fear he felt. Whoever she was, went down to the grave with his father. Now, Lorenzo searched his mind which was full, he felt his father was close.

Chapter 19. Callum's quest

Recimer, continued with, Lorenzo and Renee and a guide to the ships workings, where and what they were doing at the time. Ismondera had wanted to speak with Lorenzo at that moment also, and Callum who moments ago changed his mind to the events going on in his life because of Recimer's prior scan and teleportation of Callum aka Dennis Field and he knew why he was there and for what purposes that went deep into the structure of the business at hand that he belonged to and yet did not have full information on. Ismondera was anxious about bringing these two together, him and Lorenzo. Recimer was aware of the situation at hand but felt compelled to bring the situation to a swift conclusion. Hesitation was brought about by hand held communication devices that were hard to make out, made of light and that Recimer was now communicating on as there was also a telepathic resonance to them, all of which these devises had enabled this sort of activity as well. This bought some unexpected interest to Lorenzo and Callum (Capt Dennis). Ismondera, witnessed Callum doing the same thing and a strange sense of alertness was picked up from both groups. For Lorenzo, the white plethora of light around them somewhat changed, dimming and changing colours as the other worldly feeling changed with memories and for Callum an almost incomprehensible test for him, steadied him.

Chapter 20. Recognition of each other

Renee was asleep in her quarters, slowly she awoke. Throughout, Heniburian ship's, an electromagnetic vibration was registering at different frequencies depending on social and environmental changes, this could change and could pulse at any area and at different intervals throughout the ship. This is what monitored all life forms on the ship, a sub-conscious registry according to a person's comfort zone as the technology on the ship could assimilate thought recognition within the synapses of the brain, a matter of projected thought, this was programmed into the bio-crystalline support structure which was timed into the bio-computer crystalline frame of the ship, using quantum sized byte capacity, like that timed in to a computer. Most small gadgets were mechanically repaired if they had not been technologically grown, these were place on timing frequency alert switches, even these were registered by telekinetic telepathy by a recognized user using positive energies. These Heniburian's had the ability to project into the future to a certain point in time and space and they could move things with the use of telekinetic telepathy or power.

"Lorenzo, I now know that you've read what I think because I can hear your words."
"You've read my mind darling, I can also catch your mind projection at will but I won't at this moment." he said smiling back to Renee, "I can catch your mind projection like you can catch mine.", then Renee smiled back. "Oh don't worry, this ship does the thinking for us, when it's vital.", again smiling back. They both laughed. "There sense's must be so advanced, more than anything they've got on Earth, why is it there is no place to stay yet, surely they've found somewhere and surely there is a reason for this?" said Renee. "Yes, time is different on their ships", Inflected Lorenzo, he continued, "We are heading for their home now and what I've seen of it, God I want it to be our home!"

The light absorption rate was far higher in their craft and their world, than Earth's. The vibration energies that surrounded them were activating at a much higher frequency, these kept part of the integrity of the ship, for this is what light did, it's destination and programming was kept into account, therefore whatever food or drink was required and or offered, it would almost always be a compressed food quality type protein with pH and CO_2 water content reconstituted throughout the atmosphere, this was available from hydrator units placed on the ceiling of each level of the ship, much like a beam of energy, light would automatically carry it to the recipient. The sound waves through the curtaining of the walls also produced a field that rather than working against the body and mind, would work with it and to understand as the ship was regarded by the extraterrestrials as a body, mind and soul in itself. The psychological level was higher as too if anything was determined as out of balance, the waves could detect and project what was necessary for the recipient to recover, it was total harmony. "Yes I've seen it too, it's a beautiful place but should I be there as well?" Lorenzo said, increasing his gaze to Renee, "We belong together as far as I'm concern, you and I", pointing his finger to her, having passionately expressed this. He then looked into her eyes as he held onto her, brushing his hands down her, they kissed in what seemed an eternity.

Chapter 21. Preparations

Meanwhile on route to planet Neru, that the ship was on route to, the inhabitants were engaged in a prelude to celebrations of a ceremony, their hands did not touch but some benefited from doing this with one another, others did not. Familiar faces came to light who were, Carlos, Janice, Brine, Dalgarius and Onlio who was Lorenzo's father. "We will assist in the recovery of all groups of people who have as we've considered, called upon us in their hour of need", Alien and human alike echoed with mind telepathy and independently verbally through to the ceremonies ending, with the word "Amen" being conveyed in unison. This they did with the backdrop of the 'Crystal' city behind them.

Chapter 22. Re-union

Something began to slow in the ship, a different sound wave began to emanate. Lorenzo and Renee felt somewhat dizzy, just then Recimer and Ismondera appeared in what were the appearances of golden cloaks. Recimer began, "It is a new dawning, something we've waited for, for millennia and are now upon us, rejoice friends and I mean that! For we all will meet at last!" Ismondera approached them, "We are now slowing the ship to come in for a landing, it is your home, and please accept it this way." The light on in the ship dimmed slightly with a pulsation affect, this could be felt as they approached the planet of whose appearance shone with a lit champaign, emerald and gold colouration as if the vegetation itself was made of light. Now the ship descended through the misty light that permeated the outer shield of the planet, the red misty regions showed what looked to be pyramids, strange long buildings with translucent spirals alongside lighted buildings like crystals, all uniformly clustered together.

Chapter 23. Surveillance on the ground

Demietri also as a guide to, Lorenzo in his younger years also had known him for years before he had met Renee and had ran an antiques store close to their township, being an antiques historian and dealer as well and on this day he had a sense of dread with all the goings on in the town and so for this reason, he closed his shop. He felt compelled to go to his house as had been the case and curiosity, having taken him and he wanted to see what these particular people were up to. The neighbours of himself and Lorenzo of who had been away now for more than a week and a half and probably would never be back, unbeknown to him and with himself being none more the wiser as to what had happened to Lorenzo. Having pulled up in the car, they appeared, "I'll just check up on the back of his plantation", he thought to himself. The olives were not in season as they should have been and this normally alone had startled him, even more was the fact that he thought he saw Lorenzo, himself, thus realizing that this could be his imagination, it shocked him all the same "Or was it?" he questioned.

Looking out from the window of the house was a man of tall stature peering out at him and this raised his anxiety level a bit further. He walked a long stretch of ground to get there. He came up to the door of the house and before even knocking, this man opened the door, "Hello, what is it you want?" He had a indistinguishable accent. "I was looking around at the previous owner's house!" he said raising his voice a notch and the man mentioned to Demeitri, "To come back to the house." He had the back door open to him. Smiling now, "My name is, Menzies Karouzos, I'm friends of the tenants, Lorenzo and Renee, they are enjoying their stay here, and I'm their estate agent of Olympian estate agents. I had to leave a key for them, they trust me, they've know me for years." Menzies replied, "We...Lorenzo and I have been FRIEND'S for years, I myself used to come here quite frequently and have tried the olives in the backyard here for years.", as Demietri said this he motioned to the crop and hoped all this would intimidate this man and for some reason he felt uneasy. He smiled slightly in a way that was off hand, "Yes, yes now, if you would excuse me I have to be getting back to a few things." "You do know Lorenzo?", "Hmmm...Lorenzo who? Oh yes, yes." said Menzies, quite unready for that line of questioning. Demietri continued, "They must really trust you." Quite briskly, Menzies, now seem to want to shut the door by pushing it even closer to the door frame. "Known them for years, Goodbye." and closed the door on him, this was frustrating as there was no way to contact Lorenzo or Renee.

Demeitri was totally affixed to this estate agent and did not know anything of the estate agency this man was talking about. He remembered the brotherly trust that Lorenzo had for him as he was now thinking that foul play was at hand for Lorenzo and Renee. It was agreed upon that if something happened to either of them, that they would check up on each other as they had implicit trust of each other, this included looking after the estate and for all he knew Lorenzo, would be back but the suspicion persisted, he thought that this was peculiar, never the less he was clued up on techniques of surveillance.

He later came back that night and checked from two streets with night vision binoculars. "There's something up here, very suspicious." he said to himself. A car pulled up and two of what appeared to be women, showed up at the home, after about three minutes, another car pulled up and two men got out of the car. Demietri pulled out what was an electronics ear and pulled up a street further, this was something he used twenty years ago when he used to do security work for a high level security firm and all this techno-gadgetry was not uncommon for him to use back then. All he seemed to be picking up on was the voices muffled by some buzzing sound, whilst trying to get a read out, he detected at around four megahertz read out on his transmission spectrometer for his electronic ear. He tried getting a fix but it seem to correspond to the area itself, it manifested everywhere, however when he focused this at the imposters as he was believing, it would stay at a different fixed hertz signal, this had only increased his suspicion, he also believed the windows were fixed with vibration disrupters, so a conversation could not be heard properly and Demietri, believed more so that this was a set up, making out that not only had Lorenzo disappeared or had died but they were intending to make it clear that they were members associated with S8 for anyone who cared enough to find out and of whom, he did and Demietri but had no knowledge of them as yet. They were as he saw it now in some way responsible for the reason Lorenzo, had left, at least this is what it seemed to those around him who were the closest to him, now being Demeitri. In what Lorenzo and the others had mentioned years back and had recently told him, then this was crystallized further in his mind.

More importantly, he had been at one stage directly or indirectly employed in the security surveillance team associated with S8, he knew how they operated. He thought, "Was there an operative, a smoke screen as to what was happening in this small township?"

Chapter 24. Morphed judgment

The planet that now was inhabited by the Henuburian's was called Neru and was on the verge of one of the biggest reunions of entity energy as they the Henuburian's called it for some three thousand six hundred years and all this had been taking place over a twenty thousand year period. All this was geared through the bio-crystalline matrix that was enabled in the open for all on Neru to see and to be correlated by its craft and its computers. Cities of light, dark and matter to be managed at a cellular level and not all energy was completely this way, being an even mix of technology and bio-technology, making it somewhat a morphed reality. If the advancements were not enough for the beings on this planet, then it was considered that this new lodgement of cellular particles inhabiting their system was a telling sign that they had accepted and not rejected the new energy, for that quadrant through that time period that was part of their doctrine of politics, as they had wide ranging philosophies that they as an example as has them having mentioned, put it, "The central level core of the body, depending on its higher or lower state would correspond with this. In this case we prevail as a higher vibration form which is what these energy particles attract, our levels for growth were not just in technology, we are a technically advanced world."

Renee looked over the terrain of the planet, for the Goddess within her, she knew this was the end of the cycle of learning for her at that level, she felt her mortal coil unfold into her greater self to a new level. It was a fact that she shone greater than Lorenzo, in fact the female population on Neru, was to have a brighter aura, the light body of energy could be seen everywhere. Lorenzo would look into the depths of space. One night she asked what it was he sought, he tilted his head, paused, and turned to her..."you."

Chapter 25. Search of the Vault

Demietri, searched files over his computer and eventually discovered clues to what had bought him to this point with Lorenzo, it all pointed to the S8 team, although it wasn't called that but "operation go between". These documents he sourced from his days working in surveillance for various companies. This companies name he picked out had a security involvement in some European companies, this he thought was just not worth the effort to continue to find out, as he had dealt with other agencies which was black with a shiny surface not unlike a tile and showed all the vectors of planetary and star charts and thinking that this would help him, localize and understand something of their world. The vectors were point on any geographical surface and played a part in their overall philosophy of time and space, notwithstanding the fact that early space flight required them to possess these computers.

The slate crystal in his hand was not unlike a computer and showed the co-ordinates of home and gave him a better reference of where he was in the universe, to also interpreting thought from the viewer and could show designated material that would be helpful to the recipient. "You're at least in the vicinity of your friend's now. Welcome to your new home," said Ismondera. Demietri now had a huge smile on his face.

Chapter 26. Destruction

Meanwhile back at the village near Kalambaka, the crystal powering the time vault, powered down causing an electrical disturbance through the township and surrounding countryside, these were detected through faint signatures of light cascading in light of little pockets and distribution all over the place, causing tremors, then as the light glow faded from the crystal and it released from its foundation, causing it to crack and at many times the speed of light it headed for the ships mainframe. The labyrinth self-destructed, with the life force of light now back with the mother ship, all matter, whether crystal or metal, disintegrated in a dramatic loss of integrity in the overall structure, what followed was a massive collapse, as the vault labyrinth, fell in on itself, it was destroyed, though geologically nothing appeared to have occurred. The light glow prominence faded from the countryside and the

44

township experienced a slight tremor and was put down to nothing more than an earthquake.

Chapter 27. Recorded events

Back on the ship, the information collected from the vaults Earth history, not only helped in their knowledge of who they were but also to integrate and join the two planets in a mystical relationship, the aura of which they would both know about when they reached the summit of the pyramid, when this occurred, the two would have the kinship of both qualities that the planets possessed and so there wisdom would be combined.

Chapter 28. Celebrations

Everything had gone according to the plan and ceremony that was to take place at the arrival of all those on board the last flight in and as the crystal ship approached, Neru city, and its rendezvous with the pyramid began.

This was the day and the moment when the transition of the two planets would be finalized as the final information was flowed and integrated with their computers which were unlike Earth's and far more advanced, having their form in the pyramid. Once this was done, the messages back to the pyramids on Earth would take place and would be practically invisible to the naked eye and yet these pyramids were designed, not to what could be seen on the surface or in the air but what happened underground, as they conducted and amplified information, this was then sent to planets central core to begin work at once, to every field and vortices point on the planet, creating a planetary balance for the two millennium calendar.

Chapter 29. Atlantis

A story written by a 'UFO' journal magazine, read as follows; "It is the basis of this story, to understand deep philosophical possibilities and that of the reactions between one is covered and pioneered world to another. Politics and random supposed selection of something that has taken place almost too weird to contemplate could take place but further as to where this will lead and sightings in the regions of for example, of recent times, Southern Greece", have had the local media reporting to an extent on these sightings.

Citizens everywhere, in every country, seeing these phenomenon's of lights in the sky and strange electrical occurrences, has to postulate, "Are we not alone in the universe and will they come for those who want to see them?" This was one example of the journal reports, the second was another gazette magazine. Some of the poor media coverage of late, has a way to dissuade citizens from being overly interested in what was occurring, that it was electrical phenomenon caused through storms, etc, these are media releases revealing some of the same phenomenon, something was being stirred in people and not since the first viewing of sightings. Indeed a new wave of activity was characterized and seen by the peoples of the world and had been particularly apparent in the Baltic and Mediterranean areas, such as this type of phenomenon to the end of the story.

In Lorenzo's mind, the questions have arisen from many groups and people about a former civilization on the Earth and if this was factual evidence of the legendary civilizations like Atlantis? A couple of weeks had passed after another seeming viewing of sightings but no one picked up on it at all. Supposed missing people that had returned after many years of not being in contact, people who looked different.

For Lorenzo and Renee, for them this was now an assimilated and accepted
reality, one which had been extremely spiritual amidst all the sophisticated
technology that was involved and technology the world could be ready for, if not,
then to be spirited away for the next wave of spiritualist idea's and societies of
'vaulted time?' Atlantis was one such society to them, if not a sort of religion for some
and an obsession of dreams, a world that could have been possible? Where time,
space and reality, even fantasy, blend in and become an ensemble of universal
marvels and wonders the likes the world has never seen, yet since that time. This
was in Lorenzo's mind and more than that, he had information about the forgotten
and overlooked places of Atlantis through imparted information from the

Henuburian's, those taken on board, all did have a philosophy once lost, now as he saw, re-emerged. Lorenzo, beaconed and beseeched Ismondera and was freely to do as he felt, discharging himself from the ship after being posted on route to Earth.

Chapter 30. Broadcast from the heavens

"Light appeared in all areas of the sky and it appealed to a formerly arranged radio, even television broadcasts, with the people who appeared that way with him and to him, this literally fell to a handful of these beings, they were mostly hybrid in appearance, all Lorenzo could do was watch. In Rome there was a strange weather formation appearing above the main coliseum, one of the city's main attractions, whatever the case of these anomalies, they were appearing just about everywhere around the globe, it was occurring in Rome and Greece, however not in the same size and all major provinces and capitals.

There were saucers that appeared sporadically, everywhere, not since the large viewing of sightings in the fifties, sixties and even early seventies had this occurred. It was hard to know if they were from Earth or somewhere else. These legendary craft were sighted during the second world war but there had been sightings going back also to strange airships seen way back to the 1700's, it all played on the mind of the public. World surveillance systems were well and truly on overload and could not keep up to date with the phenomenon. On top of this, transmissions were a low quality, coverage still took place but so severe were the storms that even satellite transmissions would not be received adequately.

Chapter 31. Renee's thought's

A remarkable discovery took place for Renee. It ties in with what, Lorenzo believed to be the basis of the technology and discovery of these ancient aliens that had hid in their underground labyrinth, this is where he had uncovered this information.

Renee believed that the aliens had some technology secreted away for years and was handled carelessly but not intentionally. As members of the alien Henuburian, Recimer and Ismondera, illustrated when they celebrated the joining of two information streams into each planetary culture and this enabled balance in society, even though there is seeming upheaval. "It is problematic, that now it's seems society as a whole is falling, yes and no, what is going on is transmigration's, picture if you will a flock of geese going from one continent to another, the only one in charge is the body of that flock of geese going in that one direction, that is what the discoveries we've made have done. It's a global community but now it's time to move spiritually and physically, it's time to grow up!" Lorenzo believed that this was what was being broadcast from above this was one of the broadcast messages and very few could receive picture quality clarity pictures because of what the weather was doing.

A spokesperson from the Henuburian had been sanction by the Heniburian elders in this matter and allowed him to speak for this issue with S8 team members, this was agreed upon. He began through translation and transmission holographically, "It is now that all things are being brought into focus, it's a time to be patient, it coincides with the transmissions you are receiving, which are affecting your weather and just about everything else. Please be patient, to reveal what is happening and that a new planet is sharing itself with us, this is part of a great cycle that will take us into a further preparation of Henuburian soil." A quiet but steady applaud was heard throughout the room of S8 team security and the head of them. Dalgarius spoke for them, "We have Eastern and Western hemisphere's of the world to consider, what will happen to them in times of crisis? Financially they could go into ruin." "You now have technological, medical and financial help, we will help you." The Henuburian spokesperson at this point departed. The room went into a verbal malaise by the answer. "What light was he trying to shine?...it's been done before, war is not a means to an ends." There was some consternation in the room, then a buzzing sound that began to increase in pitch, some of them asked what was making that happen, there were some chuckles and in an instant, they all disappeared in a blinding flash as some raised their hands to their faces, this gave way momentarily to

49

a cathedral like permeation of light they were in and a cigar shaped craft's beam of light transferred them all into their ship. They had transited from Earth to a Henuburian ship and would return soon, they hovered motionless for a moment. The political situation remained stable, again after a blinding instant after just moments, some of them were back from the ship that were of the S8 security team and made a choice to return, and the others stayed. Renee had come back with Lorenzo on the return back to Earth, to help resolve with the transition which was his decision, to quest this out and had been ascertained by him, he was caught between world's momentarily. Lorenzo and Renee held hands as they looked over the city of Athens, as if saying a final farewell to the Earth.

~~~~

End of Book 1

####

New hybrid colony Book II

Nick Betar

Published by Nick Betar at LuLu

Copyright 2012 Nick Betar

Contact: c/o Australia Fair post office, Australia Fair,

Qld 4215, Australia.

Table of contents

Chapter 1.Outset to a new beginning

Chapter 2. Trick

Chapter 3. On route to Vakar

Chapter 4. Re-union of Lorenzo and Renee

Chapter 5. Ismondera

Chapter 6. Solution

Chapter 7. Drop off point, Kayelon

Chapter 8. The knowledge of the Progenitors

Chapter 9. Ismondera's intervention

Chapter 10.The significance of the numbers

Chapter 11. End of a cycle on Earth

Chapter 12. The beginning of the charting contact

Glossary of contents

Preface

The second book instalment. This reveals the next leg of the journey with these extraterrestrial beings and adventures involving the members of the of an amateur group of archaeologists and what the discoveries brought for them. Now named the 'Progenitors' and what tasks they could perform in their relationship with the Henuburians and setbacks if any were to be discovered.

Chapter 1. Outset to a new beginning

It was telepathic messages he received a reception, "Lorenzo, Lorenzo...what is it that you did with the transmogriphier" said Matorthus, the brother of Recimer, one of the full blood Henuburian and in a dialect that was rampant. "You spoke in a rampant tone, Matorthus" A transmogriphier was an apolitical correct notion of a device, capable of all nano-tech functions, which could be confusing because most instruments of the newly formed civilization of Neru and now Thelos, was back to normal and this was required of Lorenzo to use because of the adjustments made to these two planets, so that he himself could better cope and understand what was going on at a psychological and metaphysical level. For anything to have nano-functions, a categorized section, named seventy-one-zero-four-one-zero which had two of these concepts numbered and had to merge eventually with human and Henuburian thought forms, it was a type of trust mechanism, universal translator, this was an unknown concept on Earth and obviously of whom the Earth's civilization was nowhere near as technological as theirs. "Yes, I'll be right with you my friend", he replied to Matorthus. Matorthus always grafted into Lorenzo's mind, his name at the end, as if in correction and outburst to Lorenzo in front of Matorthus and with the device, held up and waving it in his hand as if to stun or seemingly incinerate him, at least in the psychological sense and Matorthus was used to sensing Lorenzo in the realm of someone with no military background but did recognise there was an understanding of some of the regimented organisation concepts of thinking in Lorenzo's mind, some of the members of the S8 team one of the security organisations on Earth, had been transported up to the one of ships, namely the 'Nop'. "Ah, you shock me" pointing his finger at Lorenzo, he continued "If this had been Earth, you would have been dead long ago." Both broke out in simultaneous laughter, in a telepathic convergence. It was not really obvious, physically it would appear as a smile and a type of postured gesturing, although sensations could be more pronounced with telepathy. Lorenzo then took an inquisitive stare at Matorthus and in an enacted civilised motioning, disengaged the handpiece he was holding and rolled it off his finger and onto the table where Matorthus was sitting. "We have fully contemplated and constabulerised", meaning (considered stable and work effective in the environment), "a hybrid counting of the records on the device and the constabularies information in this mogriphier," (formation of metaphysical field's and

52

changing them into readable data then fed to the onboard computer on the ship), "it houses all of the Earth's records and is ready for assimilation", Matorthus replied. "Don't you mean transmogriphication", inferred Lorenzo, and let out a chuckle "Yes", replied Matorthus.

They both looked out at a crystal clear backdrop of Earth's solar system's general location, beaming back as a pinprick of light amongst an array of stars, as they heading into another quadrant close to their home planet of Neru.

Chapter 2. Trick

The light from the screen was beautiful, every glistening star was its own beacon of its own apparent frequency and they could measure the energy waves in accordance with their own instrumentation and some of these stars emitted frequencies that were familiar to this new hybrid civilisation, a type of universal empathy. Thelos was in accordance with the abbreviated term, "The loss of the lost," (those who departed from times past), a civilisation who put them there aeons ago to just yesterday. Their advance in space travel, meant it could quite well be a hop, skip and a jump, this with their abbreviated phonetic and alphabets were just the tip of the iceberg for Lorenzo's understanding. Every level and discipline of mathematics and terms are interlinked with each and every phonetic alphabetical and numerological advancement. Technological instrumentations that had adaption's to interlog (log of space travel), with the ship phonetics computer system.

Micheal another assistant, was one of the ship's crew, opting to be a steward and knew his companions from Earth but only knew them first on Neru, they all kept in touch with one another and engaged in exploration with Lorenzo, as all the human passengers had the choice of doing before their discovered ascension. Delice and they were both human, was Micheal's partner and she saw in him, the fault of his ways but was more of in sympathy with him. That never went on, not after the troubles and dilemma's they went through together, now she saw an arrogance that was unlike his previous self after his evolved attitude and she was never able to ascertain whether it was to do with mathematical and grammatical calculations in his head, a frequency he had permanently latched onto, with DNA from what was delivered from the lifting, a type of hybridization? This is where a problem or a seed became apparent and whether the two thought forms were independent of one another and if it could create problems throughout or if it could truly integrate into one thought/mind. Lorenzo and Renee who was on board another ship, doing similar work and unlike, Micheal and Delice had this in their memories but so much more did Micheal and the conscious lift was far more enduring to him and believed this could help him be more than he was, it surely told in their future's that this is something they could all shine on.

Earlier in that week a being linked to the Heniburian's genetics had engaged in a rite or ceremony to bring the congregation of planets to a higher plane of existence. Earth was one more piece to the puzzle and by engaging the position they had managed. This with their records shared this to be a high chance of it to be a happening that was part of their engagement of directive of this space civilization.

Lorenzo, Delice and Micheal were the chosen catalyst's to this through the approval of Matorthus, Recimer and Ismondera, the latter alien, Lorenzo was well acquainted with and with an entire planet, (Earth) had now reached another inevitable level of existence, what with wars and environmental crises. The cataclysms on Earth had past, now the conclusion was for the continued monitoring of now the new form of life-force present there, light encapsulated in human beings. A being with a skin of light has maybe the power to transcend reality of the physical world? And such were these beings, the colonists merging had bought in on a hybrid belief system. It was inevitable and Micheal was in some thought about this. "What of this hybrid system, or Jake Jaihem, was a reality in his mind as this was and a figment of his imagination, imputing of, into a sub-system computer, sifting down and casting his eye's and turning to his holographic display, shuddering suddenly as he received a tap on the shoulder. "What is it that goes on ", whispered Lorenzo. Micheal squinted suggestively, "And the point my man...Ah ha Lorenzo, you shouldn't want to know, why, I look into this machine as I do", he stammered, shirked and smoked, what's a lie and what astrology, Lorenzo? Lorenzo turned more toward him. "I know what you want to do, is to imprint that revolting thought from Earth into the holographic and ignore largely the concept that we are trying to merge." "I don't know, Lorenzo, what are you trying to say?" "I'll be watching your progression", Lorenzo said sternly. "This Thelos, our planet of light, has been the best thing to happen to us and you do appreciate this, "I know". Micheal tilted his head downward and he squinted his eye's, pushing imaginary hair back from his bald head, in fact hair had not been growing dramatically at all for any of the males or females for that in turn was caused by the light on the ship and was full of what was termed a healthy enzyme light.

"Look, you thought I wasn't part of your grouping and this Lorenzo from the beginning", deeply sighing, Lorenzo backed up his claim. "I know you came later along with the S8." "We did know about this but allot was in theory, to which end, we go with this, we don't know", replied Mike "I trust you Mike, I have to...but if I believe there is something not right, then I will investigate, anything at all, even neurotic", On this note, Lorenzo parted taking a long hard look at the holographic, not making out the signature message that Micheal had projected into it. The room shone with a strange luminescence.

Chapter 3. On route to Vakar

The control bay was etheric (meaning ether) in its shining light, coupled by seamless decor like panels that were lighting point of light intermittently scaped by elder Henuburian plotters (pilots) large heads. Beyond laid the innumerable stars on their presage to their other planet, Vakar, pronounce, Vair ka er. Deemed to be a nursery planetoid in which the inhabitants were only vaguely aware of the presence of the outside force. It was a strangely blue with vastly more water than pre-dated, older, planet Earth, the Earth in its time-line, hosted pits and cracks, with a much darker surface, as this planetoid was lighter. The population below, unaware of anything as to their cloaked Henuburian ship, made its way into this world, a water aquatic planet. As it pulled into and through the ionic layer, it became apparent the ship was not alone but somewhat bizarre was the intrusion apparent of what would be deemed, termed, 'a sky freighter', red in colour, predominantly. Light beams shone onto the vessel. The Heniburian's, using the many seeming liquid crystal display looking controls at the helm were hit and the sound of tick and clack, were apparent with the hitting of the Heniburian ship. They stopped as a retaliatory beam was surged to their ship and it then vanished but judging from the piloteers, they knew who that was and the ship.

Vakerian people and their planet had a foreboding with their beauty, as a people they were battle ready and more in the sense that psychological informalities, could be taken as a slight, even from their own people. They had gone through great psychological upheavals and theories had been made as to whom through to the last two-hundred years, there were losses and were about and were from attacks from the ships that had been on radar and seen by the Henuburian ship, this showed up to them that they were the possible culprits of this people, the Vakars shakiness with any visitors to their planet.

The translation was" Vedgerian's, stalling us, for this territory", "We encountered and counteracted them before in all our past two-hundred years", said the Henuburian pilot. It was accepted by the new hybrid civilization, the terms and conditions of these beings from the Henuburian elder's and the pilots. These were the deficiencies of the pilots to accept to accept the term Henuburian, even though, it was their race. The belief of them being pilots prompted a meeting between specific one's to form a pact, only with knowledge known to them, with the pilot's crew scouring their eye's to the energies. They all looked out at this world's landscape, with its unusual escarpment of red and ochre, yellowish and brown rocks with second layering of mossy covering dotted around, almost like a structural landscape garden and as they approached closer, the rocks and escarpment looked more like canyons, boulder's, true like fauna, roadways, towns and cities, till finally, white speckles of birds began to appear. They were an unusual species of bird and looked a lot like a Crane or Ibis. As they drew closer to ground and descended, they were astounded, particularly to the human onboard, though not the pilots, of the technological marvel that of the space dock of their planet. Space dock approach was only five hundred yards and they could see they were a beautiful looking race of beings. They appeared non-chalant and on the ground, they would appear to have a becoming look, as they were very telepathic, a becoming look of beauty but something lurked beneath, as if haunted, hunted.

The humming beneath the craft, could be heard and felt by all on the ground, it's crystalline and metallic features present to all and then touchdown. The craft finally rested with a clinch sound and a force field de-activated, shrieked across the craft with the sound of a heavy electrical noise. Anticipation was always felt as the crew prepared to meet the inhabitants of the planet they visited. All insignia, ruffles of clothing, sheathing, were observed before stepping out to be greeting or introduced to their hosts.

From the outside, those who were greeting their visitors observed the seamlessness of the crafts door which made a 'shopping' noise as it opened, magically and noiselessly touched the ground and an eerie blue glow persisted around the edge of this door and another glow persisted as the visitors arrived from out of the craft as they then made their way down the ramp. Lorenzo, Micheal and Delice scanned the new civilisation.

The hosts were looking on with interest, some excitement and a little uneasiness and if the interest of the old Earth took away their absolute bliss in this realisation, then that these guest's had come along for the ride only made them feel for the most part, outsider's. Micheal turned to Lorenzo, "You're a bit of a worrier, and you know that, don't you?" He stopped, paused and turned to Micheal, "Well, no, I didn't know that", he said nonchalantly and with facetiousness. Micheal turned again to Lorenzo, whist they walked toward their hosts. "Let us greet them with the empathy of a human being", yes whatever grows our telepathic response is the way of the Henuburian and us, now that is."

"Greetings, we are human assistants of the Henuburian... partners with them." The Vakarian, looked on with interest and all seemed to blend into their group, then uniformly walked out and over to Micheal and Lorenzo. "Greetings, in reciprocation, we as partners of the Henuburian's believe you're come with them on a peace mission, they only ever bring other races with them as a sign that they are truly developed and care for us all as a species, and this is the way of universal principle..." Now walking over to the major cultural and commerce building that was a major monument to their political development. At this point a calm serene silence was shared with them all as the discussions continued.

The hybrid Henuburian followed behind the ordered processions of human and full Henuburian contingencies. There was brilliance in the way the procession continued and the parked visiting ship in the background with the lush growth of vegetation and the mountains on the background, capped of the whole aspect of the majestic scene, looking surreal and etheric at the same time. The apparent angels being the Henuburian beings, those that resembled the angelic presence there with their light bodies. The Henuburian had at least three types and a combination of all races full Henuburian and they only varied in height.

The consort to the host was Micheal and Lorenzo apparently equally. They had a presence of authority about them and they referred to the whole experience later on as very understanding experience between the two planetary groups and was quite sincere and revealing, this only helped the repour develop between the Henuburian and the human hybrid that were present.

Later in the evening they had arrangements for the group of humans to spend the night there, this being the first of many days they had been assigned to help with development of the civilisation and strengthen their defences against the invading forces. The name they developed for the sky or space freighter's was Molbers, these were intrusions from a variety of opportunistic retaliatory forces, much like thieves of space and their intrusions were unwarranted via the treaties that had been in existence but had been laid claim to by the intruder's his however paled by comparison to the one million years that the lawful treaty had been in force much like a baton or olympic torch, it was passed from one succeeding generation to the other.

The intercom on the helmet which was made of a lacquer like looking substance, capped off with a thin veil of shimmering light graced the human and not the hybrid or the Heniburian heads and was a deliberate and acknowledgement of the way they the Henuburian had conducted their peace time management of these and all done on these diplomatic type of procession. In the distance from the embassy and city surrounds, there was an explosion far of the left of the city named Vakar two or Vakar double as was the comparisons of language for the Vakarians. Micheal immediately consulted his radionic arm relay that had the reading for his holographic sub system computer, Lorenzo was in a momentary shocked state about the event, Vakarians scrambled about as too did some of the hybrid Henuburian. "Nice that someone was thinking of them", said Micheal in a facetious monotone of seriousness, there was the sense of compassion also in his tone, Lorenzo looked in seriousness "Another one begins", Lorenzo said with a smile. "Dad, you want me to hand this over, this I'm able to read from you", "I know my son, I know" He finally looked at and thanked Ismondera. And with his father's permission, he handed the stone to Ismondera. He held it in one hand and with the other hand cupped it, again geometrically manipulated the outside face of the pyramid computer, and again the oblong box lit up with sound and light. Onlio stood next to his son and reassured him with a hand on his shoulder as if it's alright with the revealing of their history from within the contents of the stone his father had given him.

A great smile accrued upon Ismondera's face as he continued the geometric examination and imputing with his arms and feeling the face of the computer. "Thank you, this is a blessing to you both! This concludes much of the work back on Earth, we needed a snippet of the life lead by at least some of the families on Earth and this works in with our time continuation for the computer module. I would now like the three of you to work on the project together with this computer, it will function in an important part of the life display in our biospheres and our ships. This technology will eventually be completed, Micheal are you in agreement with this", asked Ismondera

Matorthus entered the room. Going into deep thought, he concluded, "Yes, I will"
"Then that's settled. Matorthus made an announcement to the whole gathering. The pre-condition to this space excursion and all associated with have their origins in a very long history of exploration, determination and consistency of an order of thinking that has deep regard for universal function", this concluded Matorthus's statement to them and he return back to his area as quickly as he departed. Lorenzo had a question lingering in his mind and he posed it to everyone present but more meant for Micheal. "Micheal, what have you in mind for the computer data that's already in the computer?", I thought you might ask me what my intentions are or were but I think you already know, this is your project now as well Lorenzo, I wouldn't deprive you of the work of this particular project", this answer surprised Lorenzo and with that said "Yes", a slight smile emerged on Lorenzo's face, this was followed by Ismondera finishing off, what he came in the room for., though he wasn't done with Lorenzo. "Lorenzo, I have made significant changes to my DNA when I was on Earth and this was in order to make the transition from my culture to yours easier and vice versa for anyone who came through from your culture to mine. There is a lot of transparency out there in the world, if something isn't used, it dries up and withers away, but the timing was right and this alliance and travel was concluded" Lorenzo nodded his head in agreement."I thank you for your presence Ismondera, it has been quite an assignment to transmit this data to the holographic crystal pyramid computer on board.

The computer consisted of an algorithmic frequency of vibration to language adjustment, this was based on the vowels and otherwise reading of intelligent vibration of alphabetical understanding, this fit in with a type of binary coding and because the computer was in the shape of a pyramid, it did this quite accurately, geometrically and in a grid like way. It could map thought forms and chart areas of interest to the Henuburians on a longitudinal and latitudinal way as this would happen, a mind computer interface could be established, this could have differing ramifications depending on the task, thought form at hand, it could be used from an educating tool or a navigation unit for a space/star ship. Unknown to the crew, at least the human contingency was the planned use of this computer on their ship. "Ismondera, I have an idea, it was clearly outlined by the intelligence within the computer itself" Lorenzo said. Micheal was and Renee were just in sound shot of what he's telepathy, mention to him, this was frequently done when humans conversed with the Henuburians but in regards to hybrid and human, it frequently became verbalised physically through voice. Micheal then Renee followed in secession in telepathic exchange and it was quite common to take place around the frequency of ideas between public socially participating on the ships including humans, as it was seemingly easy to interface with the Henuburian when it seemed necessary as well.

"There is a seeming anomalous activity that has become noticeable to me that may or may not be noticeable to the rest as I've been monitoring the reference material on this the longest but has something to do with the mapping of new areas and it seems quite pronounced, it fits into the holographic logos of the computer and its mapping us and the material data we set forth on it in a selective but purposeful way so that its continues growing outward concentrically almost in an upward cone-shaped fashion.", Micheal reiterated. "You have outlined the main purpose and structure of the computer and its purpose", Ismondera replied, they all in the room made grimaces at each other as if they had made the discovery of a lifetime. Ismondera continued, "The computer is purposefully being programmed for your intuitive support and is a marker in an evolutionary chain of understanding for you from a universal viewpoint, the action we take is to view all the data stream from now on, it will be a participant" (as the computer was looked at as an entity from the Henuburian standpoint) "and to be integrated with the ships biospherical understanding meaning the biological knowledge and it would then participate in the directives of space travel and destination. All entities when reaching a certain stage in development would be regarded as participants. The ships analytical brain had further compartments that would house extra civilisation viewpoint cultures that would be vacant for this integration to occur and build around it like a flower, so it was now time, you will be the first progenitors of the growth and knowledge of this computers knowledge and feeling, the requirement of this will be to help over view the computers growth and development", this concluded what he was saying and they all nodded their heads in agreement.

They and the Human contingent left to Kayelon and the duties of data transference and knowledge collection took place, following the similar functions of repeating of diplomacy and spending several days on their planet securing trust and help, they left on the Nop, starship.

Chapter 4. Re-union of Lorenzo and Renee

The passenger star ship called Margel pronounced Maa-g eil had docked beside the Henuburian star ship Nop, as soon as this was done it returned to the next neighbouring sector some four million light years away. The ship Nop had unlike some of the other star ships, a trans-dimension skin that could adhere to quantum travel through worm holes and such through the fabric of time and space, this was all controlled through all the ships central core as these ships were alive and could interface with their passengers on a regular basis. Every ship had its own personality and this influenced how this all was regulated, they would heal too, although there would be specific applications for the techniques to be applied to these ships. Crystal's could be introduced to assist this process, upgrades to the ships sometimes required an interface with pilots and its computer functions and Renee had just been on a job with them. Job was the specific name of the co-alliance with ship agenda and its hierarchy of passengers. Much of it was on an equal footing but at times it took, main agents, usually the full Henuburian that were specifically applying the focus of the work and its agenda. Renee had partaken of these as well as her friends Sandriea, Suiga, Dolly and Beaunia, from back on Earth.
They were all to partake in the expeditions in space time. They were the representatives of a galactic explorative community.

Micheal had set up the holographic computer. A representative wanted to familiarise Lorenzo and Renee but to an extent, the computer project was left in the hands of Micheal and the Henuburians wished it that way, however he wanted the company of Lorenzo in particular with him on this, it was a strangely silent experience to be around the device. There were anomalies of light that were perceived or seen physically around it and ionisation could occur though on a small level. A treaty had been set up through the Henuburian that required every person human or otherwise, that if they wanted to see, hear investigate or collect data and information from it, it required that it go through Micheal always, as he was the one responsible for its data and maintenance.

Chapter 5. Ismondera

"Micheal, Lorenzo, Renee come with me", said Ismondera one of the arch instigators of the combining of Earth's 'time vault' crystal and Neru's information crystal geographies from a previous trip from Earth of which Lorenzo and Renee had taken direct part in. The crystal Lorenzo had obtained from his father Onlio since a last visit to Athens had now but played its entire part in the crystal of the time vault on Earth and Neru's crystal which was larger and had an interface ready with Lorenzo's dark crystal. Lorenzo had all but forgotten it and new that something had to be done eventually with this collector of information.

Standing beside the pyramid computer, a strange benevolence could be felt and the computer was 200 years in the making of its history, Ismondera address them from the other end of the computer. "Lorenzo, you have served well on our expeditions and demonstrated valour in the journey you took with all your friends equally. So this next request should come as no surprise, we will need the information on the crystal your father found all those years ago, all the information on there will be sufficient to finish the computer information instalments. Lorenzo, stood in utter amazement that Ismondera could request such a thing, almost like a shock to him! I'm troubled by this Ismondera, you see my father years ago told me how you or myself could be placed into a position..." Ismondera interrupted. "Lorenzo, I understand though we will need your father here as well", "I see, Ismondera", said Lorenzo, in an urgent tone. "We'll help you, it is Henuburian property, every crystal found in that cave back on Earth was related to the work we were doing" Ismondera continued. "With Ismondera's eight arms, he proceeded to touch and geometrically guide his hands over the pyramid, the oblong box in front of it exploded into colourful synchronic tone and light, the smooths sides of the pyramid went from beige to a luminescent grey colour and began to pulse. A feeling of bliss and wonder touch the air. "It's radiating the universal beacon for the planet Vakar, this helps their civilisation to grow, there are platforms for the work we do and our race has a part as well as the hybrids and humans, they learn from us as do we learn from them! Every little bit of information has its role in the agenda."

Onlio was called onto their space ship following several hours, he had finished a journey on the other side of the star system they were in which was in another star system, known on Earth as Canes major. This time it was just Onlio Lorenzo, Micheal and Ismondera, Renee was back with the friends in there quarters. "Ismodera preceded, "Onlio what is your wish about the crystal you gave your son back on Earth?" That Lorenzo is to keep ...it" Onlio knew what this was about and nodded to Lorenzo and said, "Lorenzo my boy, you know that when one cycle ends, another one begins", he said with a smile. "Dad, you want me to hand this over, this I'm able to read from you", "I know my son, I know" He finally looked at and thanked Ismondera. And with his father's permission, he handed the stone to Ismondera. He held it in one hand and with the other hands, again geometrically manipulated the outside face of the pyramid computer, and again the oblong box lit up with sound and light. Onlio stood next to his son and reassured him with a hand on his shoulder as if it's alright with the revealing of their history.

A great smile accrued upon Ismondera's face as he continued the geometric examination and imputing with his arms and feeling the face of the computer. "Thank you, this is a blessing to you both! This concludes much of the work back on Earth, we needed a snippet of the life lead by at least some of the families on Earth and this works in with our time continuation for the computer module. I would now like the three of you to work on the project together with this computer, it will function in an important part of the life display in our biospheres and our ships. This technology will eventually be completed, Micheal are you in agreeance with this", asked Ismondera

Matorthus entered the room. Going into deep thought, he concluded, "Yes, I will", said Micheal. "Then that's settled. Matorthus made an announcement to the whole gathering. The pre-condition to this space excursion and all associated with have their origins in a very long history of exploration, determination and consistency of an order of thinking that has deep regard for universal function", this concluded Matorthus's statement to them and he return back to his area as quickly as he departed. Lorenzo had a question lingering in his mind and he posed it to everyone present but more meant for Micheal. "Micheal, what have you in mind for the computer data that's already in the computer?", I thought you might ask me what my intentions are or were but I think you already know, this is your project now as well Lorenzo, I wouldn't deprive you of the work of this particular project", this answer surprised Lorenzo and with that said, a slight smile emerged on Lorenzo's face, this was followed by Ismondera finishing off, what he came in the room for., though he wasn't done with Lorenzo. "Lorenzo, I have made significant changes to my DNA when I was on Earth and this was in order to make the transition from my culture to yours easier and vice versa for anyone who came through from your culture to mine. There is a lot of transparency out there in the world, if something isn't used, it dries up and withers away, but the timing was right and this alliance and travel was concluded" Lorenzo nodded his head in agreement."I thank you for your presence Ismondera, it has been quite a journey but I had faith that this would present as a solution and a dead end."

Chapter 6. Solution

The ship jeered toward the Alpha Centauri star system and had made a new heading, one that required an intercept to do with Vakar's history time line. The time line was dotted in one area with the development of the Molbers freight ships or any ship that had an inclination at theft of planetary resources. The ears of every Henuburian telepathically heard the message, which was recorded on a frequency that had been broadcast physically this way to enhance the information being received by Human and Hybrid alike.

Meanwhile in the pilot quarters, the ship had made an interception of a number of space freighters, all appeared to be Molbers, the Henuburian ship was cloaked but in some circumstance they de-cloaked to threaten these Molbers not to be in the area and to disperse from the area. It was not permitted to be there as they had a time-line reference from where they had been and that was in the vicinity of a nebula the Henuburians had been monitoring but looking out for the Kayelon, a planet with many moons, seven in all, making it the biggest and most notable in that solar star system and within the Andromeda sector of space "Vectors are set and the course will be heading", said the pilot Manderell, to pilot Locor all was imputed instantly into directional computers and the course was begun. If anything, there was an apparent stand-off, Locor explained to Manderell, Ismondera was called to the piloting room even though he was making his way there. "Door", and it opened as the door was always sealing for the pilots and a correct mind frequency opened them, this was true of any secure room part of the ship that the pilot (piloteering) room was one of them. "What have you found" replied Ismondera to Locor, "Some sort of discrepancy that's anomalous with these Molbers freighters, ten of them left but these four have not taken flight as yet with two disappearing down a space time tunnel, the other left with an auto warping flight and the door to the room dematerialised and materialised again with Matorthus now entering , radionics and crystalline responding were momentarily disrupted and light carrier waves as well" reasoned Matorthus, "Yes, I noticed a slight disruption with key in," ('key in' was part of the analogue to the piloteers flight controls) "and a drop in gravitational pressure" Light barriers were then activated, first personally around the individuals in the ship and a stasis mode for the ship as it deployed an intensive shield around it.

Up ahead was a black hole detected some 1500 kilometers from the ship, then one of the two Molbers ships exploded. "A distress message automatic from the Henuburian ship and by the crew telepathically, let the other passengers mostly hybrid and the small content of human on board know that an attack or until otherwise known, had taken place." It was registered by the ship as a seven kiloton blast and by me eight point five", replied Manderell. Locor measure it at seven as did Ismondera and Matorthus, "Well let's find out how she is, a term they had used for the ship and engaged in telepathic response. The ships bio-crystalline support structure and computer, (not the one being programmed by now, Micheal, Lorenzo and Renee though needed attention) was alright , it only needed attention in the core and outer areas of the ship. "These thieves are getting bolder", said Locor, "Yes we

67

have to make some serious decisions on this, replied Matorthus. The pilot Manderall pull away from the black hole and tried sealing it back up, then recanted on this as the other ten Molbers had flown down it and had be artificially made, if they closed it wouldn't be in treaty with them as preserving life was the necessary requirement of them. Then all of a sudden it closed. "Well the universe made a decision on that one Manderall" said Locor.

"I'll see how everyone is "Matorthus replied and left the room, Manderell turned to Ismondera smiled and gestured that he should get into the pilots chair. Ismodera accepted. "You have been making good progress on the Holographic computer project with Micheal haven't you?" said Manderall. I have been involved in four of these types of projects and have not had too many difficulties with this, I just hope that the bio-crystalline structure and integrity hold all the thought-forms as before in the computer there working on", melancholy proceeded his words, "you'll get back into the piloteering room again, I assure, it was a close shave but we'll make it!" Locor put his hand on Ismondera's shoulder reminding of his days when he used to pilot the ship before accepting the time vault project Ismondera and Manderall closed in on the destination towards the planet 'Kayelon' as they looked out toward a vast star system with nebulas up ahead Tears were different for the Henuburians.

Chapter 7. Drop off point, Kayelon

Intensive activity was reported and recorded around the solar star system of the planet Kayelon, a planetoid that was strangely organic with dark continental surfaces of green and brownish textures. It was to the Henuburian a universe that to them was like an adventure playground though they treated their work with diplomacy and seriousness as back home in Neru they answered to a high command that regarded their work as if it were for passing any school exams for graduation. There cargo was technological and organic for this particular planet and would enhance their bio systems and technology, all of which could be grown. The civilisation was always happy to have contact with the Henuburians. Cloaking was necessary with some of the planetary civilisations that they visited and assisted as attack from the likes of the Molbers (space freighters) and others could come about.

There was the crew always to assist, on this assignment to diplomacy with the Kayelon high command and other diplomats, via the hybrid humans and human occupants on board. Micheal, Lorenzo and Renee were assigned to the recording of their assignment to transmit this data to the holographic crystal pyramid computer on board.

The computer consisted of an algorithmic frequency of vibration to language adjustment, this was based on the vowels and otherwise reading of intelligent vibration of alphabetical understanding, this fit in with a type of binary coding and because the computer was in the shape of a pyramid, it did this quite accurately, geometrically and in a grid like way. It could map thought forms and chart areas of interest to the Henuburians on a longitudinal and latitudinal way as this would happen, a mind computer interface could be established, this could have differing ramifications depending on the task, thought form at hand, it could be used from an educating tool or a navigation unit for a space/star ship. Unknown to the crew, at least the human contingency was the planned use of this computer on their ship. "Ismondera, I have an idea, it was clearly outlined by the intelligence within the computer itself" Lorenzo said. Micheal was and Renee were just in sound shot of what he telepathic mention to him, this was frequently done when humans conversed with the Henuburians but in regards to hybrid and human it frequently became verbalised physically through voice. Micheal then Renee followed in secession in telepathic exchange and were quite common to take place around the frequency of ideas between parties participating on the ships including humans as it was seemingly easy to interface with the Henuburian when it seemed necessary. "There is a seeming anomalous activity that has become noticeable to me that may or may not be noticeable to the rest as I've been monitoring the reference material on this the longest but has something to do with the mapping of new areas and it seems quite pronounced, it fits into the holographic logos of the computer and its mapping us and the material data we set forth on it in a selective but purposeful way so that its continues growing outward concentrically almost in an upward cone-shaped fashion.", Micheal reiterated. "You have outlined the main purpose and structure of the computer and its purpose", Ismondera replied, they all in the room made grimaces at each other as if they had made the discovery of a lifetime. Ismondera continued, "The computer is purposefully being programmed for your intuitive support and is a marker in an evolutionary chain of understanding for you from a universal viewpoint, the action we take is to view all the data stream from now on, it will be a participant" (as the computer was looked at as an entity from the Henuburian standpoint) "and to be integrated with the ships biospherical

understanding, (meaning the biological knowledge) and it would then participate in the directives of space travel and destination. All entities when reaching a certain stage in development would be regarded as participants. The ships analytical brain had further compartments that would house extra civilisation viewpoint cultures that would be vacant for this integration to occur and build around it like a flower, so it was now time, you will be the first progenitors of the growth and knowledge of this computers knowledge and feeling, the requirement of this will be to help over view the computers growth and development", this concluded what Ismondera was saying and they all nodded their heads in agreement.

They and the Human contingent left to Kayelon and the duties of data transference and knowledge collection took place, following the similar functions of repeating of diplomacy and spending several days on their planet securing trust and help, they left on the Nop, starship.

Chapter 8. The knowledge of the Progenitors

The mission of the Henuburians and their circuit to Vakar and Kayelon was in part to do with the development, not only of the Human and hybrid cultures and civilisations on board but the same with those civilisations they visited and monitored. Renee had put just as much in if not more in the development of the computer as Lorenzo had and had actually completed the task quicker with more information streaming going from their minds, than Michaels in the past several days they were participating. Packets of the information stream were fed into the

other cultures in prepatory or in preparation, the visits from them via their computer data base. Renee and her friend's transferred to the "Iscantor", another star-ship in the quadrant of the Andromeda, they, Lorenzo and Renee agreed that from time to time, they should separate on different missions through the job notion that was agreement through universal principles of the Henuburians job, being the mission at hand but because of technology their being apart was not as really a long time apart at all, they could join up within the time frame of the missions they undertook and the time difference weighed up by the circumstances, the velocity of the ships was another time factor cut down that they could meet more often.

Progenitors was their name from then on, it would be looked at as the insignia they could place on their uniform apparel. The need to follow procedure and function was well outlined, anything introduced was quarantined and either recognised as a further thought form development into the introduction of a suitable function within the ship.

The progenitors were Micheal, Lorenzo and Renee, they had the option of following the introduction of the "Job" and the capacity of the ship from a directive point of view to add another grouping on to them and as this was now considered by Lorenzo and Micheal, they finally left it up to Renee who decided that her friend's who she knew and were close childhood friends, that after being delivered from the veritable trouble back on Earth and after having left the star ship Margel, that being Sandriea, Dolly, Beaunia and Suiga and this made the company now, five females and two males.

It was a foregone conclusion, that no threats to security of the ship was a problem on board and that the crew had all past the trust of the Henuburian and the idea was telepathically agreed to by Ismondera and Matorthus, that they should get all the crew together to meet in the reception bay of the ship. Everyone including the pilots came along, this was to get an understanding between everyone, what the protocol was and what they had further to do. The ship was on auto control of the ships main bio-crystalline computer, which now had the streaming of the 'progenitors' bio-crystalline pyramid computer all of which was placed into a balance effect of computer integration and assimilation. Once every crew member had entered the room the reception, it began. "Greetings all crew member participants, you have been given a great opportunity to participate and because you have reached a certain level of understanding, you will have the undulating, applaud and honour of such" said Galmeda, a Henuburian elder, an applaud rang out from the crew. He continued, "because of this participation, you will receive knowledge and understanding, further your space exploration and you will be bestowed with these gifts of the universe," another applaud and cheering, the room was electric. His tone became solemn. We have the most protective up to strength, technology you could find and your cares will be taken care of. It is for this reason, that if you are caught in any perilous action, you will have the protection of this fleet. We have your cultural actions now integrating with this ship gesturing to Michael, Lorenzo, and now the most recent additions Renee, Sandriea, Dolly, Beaunia and Suiga, that made up the 'Progenitors'. Another applaud rang and some cheering, the elder then acknowledged the rest of the crew members. This concluded the gathering and everyone dispersed from there.

Ismondera, walked over to Lorenzo and Renee. Renee was set to depart back to the Margel star ship through teleport, sometimes they docked with the ships when there was a possible manual type of problem. "Can you come with me, I want to tell you what is on arrival, your planet again, your set to deliver a signalling transfer of data from the computer and then we touchdown and then we'll begin diplomacy. It will be the year 2025 and I expect you'll have guessed we've crossed over the time zones a bit, Ismondera said with a grin, Lorenzo laughed as did all the group once they heard about it.

Their path was set and they attempted to contact the necessary diplomatic representatives back on Earth of that time period, they were going to bring the same technological data that was meant for the time period and diplomatic relations had been set up many years before. This was going to be a rendezvous back to Earth to remember as this was a time period they had not even seen for their planet eager to see what changes had taken place so were anxious to know. Making this time jump was not too hard for the Henuburians as this was what they were akin to doing with their star ships. A representative was sent off and the diplomatic entourage was ready to touch down and transfer data and record with one another, this had to be done form the ground as this was always the affirmed process of sending information with one ground person to the ship and it was also what they were used to and the development of off world planetary dialogue was based on cultural interpretation but the human crew assessing the development along with some hybrid human still had a task of a job learning the cultural changes to a future planet Earth. They all stayed for several days as was the usual time allowance for each planet but only at intervals were they required for months at a time. Suiga had discovered and had trained sufficiently as had the rest of the newly required crew of the Progenitors. She detected through mind and technology causatives a monstrous anomaly with the stream of data that had either been interrupted or was tainted by an energy binary field within the scope of the data transferred to and from the ship and their data collectors. This then was picked up from the rest of the group and immediately processed and analysed so that it could be screened and to remove the infected data. For the Henuburian this had occurred previously and so the idea of sabotage had occurred from a suspected Molber ship. Indeed it had been prior to their arrival to Earth's atmosphere that the suspect anomaly though cloaked registered on the Nop's detectors. The Molber's had been perfecting their cloaking abilities and this was sometimes difficult to detect from Henuburian ships, sort of like closed circuit television footage, it had to be manually scanned to be sure what it was.

"Alert status we have an anomalous data entry, Locor", mention the ship, Nop's data banks. "Thank you very much Nop", she replied to the ship, "Your welcome Locor", it responded. She had the main job of intercepted data streams but was the responsibility of every being, particularly the Henuburians on board any of their ships and there was a detected virus in the data load, now being corrected and verified by Locor.

The representatives, ambassadors and the all human progenitors had delivered supplies, data streams and comfort to those they had met during their stay on future planet Earth. What an orchestration of events that followed, they were met by those of whom had abilities in the arts. A good dialogue had taken place and there had been no resistance to what was shared.

An agreement took place between Lorenzo and Renee at this time, they had some issues to contend with and had expressed it between each other.

Chapter 9. Ismondera's intervention

It was at this time that there was no dialog shared with any of the on board Henuburians, there was a perception that something had been going through the mind of a particular grouping, specifically Lorenzo and Renee. They had been a couple back on Earth that had seem to share the same view point and were of the same mind in regards to future events, this had been the capability of the Henuburian to know. Ismondera did know them and had taken them through certain areas of the Labyrinth whilst they had waited for a time as they had done during the process of coming through the tubes of light. Some of the beings on Earth had tried to intervene by exploring the Labyrinth, though the motives may have been somewhat different to what the Henuburians had considered normal.

Micheal follow Lorenzo into the room Ismondera had been whilst in his hibernator, a sleep bed. He had awakened and stood up in the presence of Lorenzo and Micheal. "Ismondera, I need to speak with you", "Yes, you would like to go back, Lorenzo", his hybridised features contorted as he said this to him. "Yes", Lorenzo replied back and Micheal took his cue, to leave the room, nodding his head. Ismondera approached the light of the room made him appear angelic, though all of the Henuburian were angelic in appearance."You have to follow the directive Lorenzo, you and Renee until we touch down again" he paused "We have a certain time and range to work in we will let you go and then we will be in contact with you still." he said this to Lorenzo with his hand on his shoulder. "She should be here...back soon and then I will tell her the news" Ismondera smiled at Lorenzo. "He considered the situation and realised that he wanted to still be in the employ of the Henuburian, he knew he would always be in contact with them, though he had his doubts, he knew they would keep in touch and come through for Ismondera at least and follow along. Ismondera realised there was more to discuss to Lorenzo about his past and that this was not the time to let him feel as if he wasn't in complete control of his life, though indeed he was, it was the fact that the displacement of mind and different capacity of thought that he felt he needed to take leave of and go about his natural life and even though he had come out of a great calamity of events, this is what he felt to do. Ismondera agreed and he went straight a rendezvous point with Renee. He felt all the protocol of thought, the actions and the veritable typesetting of mind were becoming more apparent to him as he honed in on the fact he was already contemplating the different lifestyle out of the Henuburian company and this with Renee, it would be just as it was again in his life.

He fell into his spell hand in hand with Renee looking at their telepathically chosen and verbalised agreement with the Henuburian in the contemplation of leaving the reality they were in! It was what Ismondera knew was best for the time being though he would miss his friends, he knew they would still have an unbroken link forever more with them. The planet seemed to sparkle all the colours of the time period and it had changed dramatically to them, this was going to be their home again with all the arrangements made prior to on the ground through a contact of theirs.

An almost surreal presence and landscape opened up before them, it was what they wanted, a new start on the prairies of an isolated area, perhaps being regarded by anyone who met them in this arrangement as an eccentric couple. Waving goodbye to Ismondera, the ships translucency going from blue to pink red and green in it pyramid form slowly disappeared from site. They were standing there stunned for a moment, and then turned to each other in a flicker of growing recognition. Renee rested her head, amidst the residence they had acquired, there contacts had been made prior to from people they knew from the time period of this Earth they were now bound by. They lived and worked in the prairie regions just outside of the Alaskan wilderness and this suited them well. There research from their past excursion with the Henuburians was still continuing and this was always followed up by communication between him and Ismondera.

Chapter 10. The significance of the numbers

Lorenzo, Lorenzo! Renee had been talking to a local in the area, Margaret, their neighbour had an agricultural seed developing and fruit and vegetable business that had been their interest for quite some time as they were a couple with Ted as her partner. Margaret explained a type of grape that was hardy to all conditions of weather and could be grown even in regions of Alaska, though it was still in its development stage it was near close to being the perfect regional grape for the area. Renee continued, "Lorenzo, our neighbour is growing grapes here in Alaska". "Wow, how were they able to do that?" he retorted, "Well, go see them, they're a couple and they do things unconventionally", Renee gave a chuckle and Lorenzo gave a smile, "Of course they do, they're just like us!" Lorenzo said.

This prompted him to walk over and to get in contact with them. Margaret was there and told him roughly the same thing as Lorenzo. Margaret and Ted eventually invited them to come over and vice versa. With Lorenzo's interest in the grape and vineyard scene of course all of this interested him and eventually they both wanted to do the same and grow vineyard in Alaska!

A few days later Lorenzo asked Renee about the progenitors project they were involved with and questioned whether this had anything to do with the idea, that any amount of transfer stream information went from their subconscious and into any transferred data stream that went to Earth this was a usage of numbers, this was the perception that it was possible and that they fit into certain geometries of the universe for instance single double, triple and quad and so on figures. They considered this seriously and thought that maybe the next time they contact Ismondera which was with a communicator device, it had a type of pin regalia looking insignia that could be attracted to clothing, they had them usually on their collar or vice versa they would find out if this was related. The next day, they did get a call from Ismondera and to their astonishment and amazement this was so. "You have linked into the synchronicity of the thought forms and whilst you were in agriculture, your thoughts honed in on the data streams that you attracted and there, you became your experience" Lorenzo chuckled, "Sounds very Zen doesn't it", Ismondera responded. "I miss the assignments you know" "Yes, we know and there will be a time when you and Renee will come back but you are both better off on the ground at this point and would prefer you did things this way for now. It suits you I know. We'll be in touch friend, again soon" "Bye for now, Lorenzo" "Bye for now"

The grapes were starting to grow in their patch of the garden and this was how they started there co-op and amalgamated grape growing between them and to produce the grapes for that region and then Lorenzo let rip on the history he shared with Renee and what significance this meeting with him was most probably all about to Ted, Margaret partner.

"Lorenzo, you must be crazy for me to believe what you've spoken of to me. Those lights in the Mediterranean were the craft of a race of beings that have been here for

78

millennia?"And the interference that was created by all of this was all over the world, was due to theses beings?" He began to walk off, he paused then stopped. "You know the thought is extraordinary but what would they want here and why?" "They were here to save and guard the planetary body from harm, like a child which is humanity when it is needing help from a parent, this is what they have been here for, I won't bring this up again", he replied to Ted. Both went back to the vineyard testing results they had been working on, and Lorenzo related that he had spoken of their contact with the extraterrestrials, Renee was unimpressed with this mention of this but seemed quietly accepting of the idea of what Lorenzo had said. "We could be hounded again, we can't risk this Lorenzo, remember what we went through before!" "I know darling, I wouldn't do anything I don't think wouldn't be accepting of Ismondera."

It was a week later and it was if there had not been a word said about the expeditions Lorenzo and Renee had taken, except for the occasional odd look they considered them either eccentric or a possible hallucinations, besides, the vineyards had grown exceptionally for the climate and this diverted their angst against this show of perceived eccentricity "Lorenzo, how these vineyards are taking shape, I'm still in disbelief but I must be believing in this because look how well we are doing!", remarked Ted. Before Lorenzo could utter another word, the din of the Nop overhead had come over and created a vibration and came into view for only a few seconds and then disappeared. To the gaze of Ted and later followed by Margaret, who caught a tail end glimpse of it. "What was that, Ted!?" Ted immediately looked over at Lorenzo and now with Renee, "I guess we're convinced now as to what is going on with you guys" He smiled broadly at Lorenzo and Renee, Margaret placed her hand assuring on Ted's shoulder. To Lorenzo, this was the right time to go into further dialogue concerning the expeditions he and Renee had taken and both Lorenzo and Renee explained further and in more detail as to what they had experienced.

Chapter 11. End of a cycle on Earth

Like the cycles to a season, so too the cycles of the stay on Earth that any of the Progenitors had on the Earth sphere. Their work entailed a higher calling and whether it had been the last physical stand of Lorenzo and Renee, the question seemed to be what they thought was happening and this was the fact that they had come to the end of the cycle of their learning on Earth. They were called to a higher calling and in the continuance of understanding the part they played, including the now interested Ted and Margaret.

It was the following week that Ismondera had concluded the charting the Earth's sector of space and it was the spaceship Nop's continuance of charting and contacting civilisations into the next area of space, this would prove more challenging but Lorenzo had accepted the idea, and it would be two years since they had been returned to Earth. After tearful goodbyes, with their neighbours Ted and Margaret, the Nop ship made its appearance with its glistening blue base and colourful metallic pyramid structure Lorenzo and Renee were beamed on board in a flash of light witnessed only by their neighbours. Ismondera Matorthus and Locor, the ships analyst of data made an agreement through Lorenzo and Renee with their permission, to keep in contact with them and the property they left was kept and looked after by their Ted and Margaret. It took the couple a while to get over the arrival of the ship and the leaving of the couple in a flash of light but they would be in contact.

Chapter 12. The beginning of the charting contact

It was now that the new expedition was to take place and they would leave for the sector in human's terms or in Henuburian terms, the end of mapping Intergalactic A is the first letter, as this is how they perceive the alphabetical response to the area of universal mapping.

The protocols had been given to the couple by Ismondera. Some familiar people had come to greet them indeed member s of the Progenitors. Michael and his wife, Delice along with Suiga and Sandriea, girlfriends of Renee. Dolly and Beaunia had posted onto another assignment but would return to the Progenitors project, it was agreed to be assigned for a lifetime.

They re-entered an area of space that was neutral, the farthest away from planetary bodies and suns as possible and in the direction they were going, to engage in the new area space charting and contacting. Sector z, was being initiated, with communications toward that quadrant of space being made before any arrival. They gave it about a week in Earth time to re-establish vectors and begin the journey. It would be a journey of about a hundred million light years before they got toward their first post, where communication grappling (deciphering would take place).

Depending on the amount of time it would take at least ten weeks to understand any language well in theory. Everything was geometrically understood in the universe. Prologue of pilots and ship Nop's record in Henuburian terms was 00.00.0000 sector convergence. Matorthus and Locor signalled to the pilot after translating the ship

Nop's data entries. It was ready to go, as the ship began to glow a golden rainbow of colour, the blue base a bright bluish colour, it set off for Intergalactic B, the second letter in the alphabet or the second quadrant to be explored and mapped. In the blackness of space, its body of light moving forward into a slowly energising charge set off like a beacon to that area of the galaxy in a magnificent flash of light.

~~~

End of book II

Thank you for reading my book 'New Hybrid Colony Book II'
For further information and updates, please write to the author at the following address; Nick Betar, c/o Australia Fair post office, Australia Fair, Qld 4215 Australia.

####

On approach to Quadrant B. Darlapaatha-a Book III

Nick Betar

Published by Nick Betar at LuLu

Copyright 2013 Nick Betar

Contact: c/o Australia Fair post office, Australia Fair,

Qld 4215, Australia.

~~~

Table of contents

Chapter 1.New ground, new space
Chapter 2.A banding of ships
Chapter 3.The presage and procedure
Chapter 4.Disaster strikes
Chapter 5.Rapture
Chapter 6.Irreconcilable logic
Chapter 7.Questions and answers
Chapter 8.Touchdown and final resonance
Chapter 9.Interaction
Glossary of contents

Preface

In the third book instalment, members of the alien star ship, Nop are beginning
the mission directive to explore the new quadrant sector as yet largely unsearched,
physically if only to start with their vibration and attuning scan devices to see where
they are. Going by their understanding as yet of the cosmos with mapped area's
ranging from the centre of the galaxy to other sectors and quadrants further afield,
this is the start of a new presage of discovery even for the Henuburian's as they
embark on an entirely new area of space, geographically and politically.

Chapter 1. New ground, new space

Lorenzo dreamt of the meandering prairies of the Alaskan wildness he had left a
week earlier, still getting over the hang-over of change from a while on the Earth life.
He started to shift in an uncomfortable manner, a sheet twisted around his ankle and

his eye's popped open, "Where the hell are we!" He murmured into a shout. The sheet he unravelled around his foot and he discerned a feeling he had not felt since he'd been aboard on the Nop, indeed any star ship of the Henuburian's civilization as his hang over of Earth cleared. The wayward subtle sounds and feeling of the ship made indistinguishable tones and sounds that he was still half awake to. On approach to the door of his room, a command to open telepathically did not move it, at least the delay was two seconds. Lorenzo followed the facade galley ways of the ship, that always had an ornate structure as simplistic and technologically sophisticated as any ship builder could anticipate to do, sleek tones of glimmering metals called blasaleded by the Henuburian's was much like those seen back on the base of Ismondera's labyrinth back on earth, structures and materials able to withstand great impacts.

A sound began to emanate from a section of the ship that Lorenzo was familiar with and having passed a number of the crew and greeting them was met by Suiga, friend of Renee. She came up greeting Lorenzo with a large smile, "If you're looking for Renee, she was dispatched to the other ship Margel," (pronounced Maa-g-eil), "she should be back in two days" "Why did she go, it's seems a little unlike her", he said lifting an eyebrow. Suiga smiled back, "She's a big girl, she will be alright." "That must be why I awoke with a start" said Lorenzo and he laughed, so did Suiga. "It must be this new sector, it's playing with onboard sychometery (a word used to describe in Henuburian terms, a psychological understanding by the onboard computer brain for the ship). She raised all her fingers to her head in a gesture that it was all in the mind, Lorenzo grinned again." Want to follow up on the Progenitors project?" He asked. "I was just following up on it. And now that the data pyramid had been installed, the others are joining the databank boxes and pyramids and are part of the project and it required that they hold a new wand type implement to shine a data retrieval back and forth", she replied back. As an example it could be a memory or an piece of historical information and that could include any type of information that was regarded with interest particularly from a diplomatic perspective, then uploaded via the onboard computer brain for analysis.

They began their session activities with that of data assimilation from retrieval and this included the ships computer system, taking up data and disseminating the information. The entire time usually took from one to two hours depending on the amount of information and how it had been stored or retrieved. Some retrieval based on the severity of the retrieval was put to the test some times. All of this could have led many investigations but time was of the essence to catalogue and continue. As this continued the colour defragmentation was more discriminated and acute than usual on the sides of the of the data box and pyramid where information was lodged, the reason being that the quadrant had reset the computer data base to create more space thereby making any information take a download more easily and this had not happened often.

A registering beep could be heard through all retrieval systems through the ship and a significant load of information had picked up on and disseminated space frequencies that convoluted into an intelligent message frequency and these more often than not were picked up on the Henuburian databases, once transferd they were deciphered and a proper reading could take place of the frequency or frequencies that more often than not had glitches throughout and could be seamlessly joined to get a more accurate deciphering.

"Hi there, Lorenzo!" responded Delice, Micheal's wife. "Hi Delice, how is your morning", Lorenzo proceeded to wave out, and Suiga did the same. Micheal then entered the room with her. "Micheal, Delice!" Lorenzo waved as if to come over and say something and investigate, they all were prone to do as part of the Progenitors group. "See this?"Pointed out Lorenzo to all present and on seeing Micheal, who was the first of that group and had a very strong grasp of the whole project, though Lorenzo did have his doubts at first, he continued, "This is the issue I've noticed with the pyramid and the data stream going into this pyramid and is now retrieved as more pronounced and has this pyramid going off like a Christmas tree", he said laughing, as it was a pun that had stereotypically taken up as almost comedic amidst an alien civilization. "I know this Lorenzo, I've accounted for this too, I think it has something to with the master computer onboard and how it is accessing the stream at the present through its holographic display and just how it's retrieving information and this fits in with the journey at hand", said Micheal, and turning to Lorenzo and Suiga seriously, he continued "We are heading to another quadrant and what Matorthus has told me and others of the Henuburian's crew, it's hard to know, there light platform is very complex, as you know it's very hard to know fully what they do, so just accept what this has for us at the moment."

A notification message had arrived to the Nop from star ship CO or just C-O, standing for the pronunciation of two planets in the history of the Henuburian's called Calla and Optomiox both now disintegrated through a solar collapse in the Andromeda galaxy. A broadcast was made throughout the Nop of the passenger arrival and transfer from the CO to the Nop star ships. Included were two of Renee's friend's Sandriea and Dolly, Beaunia who stuck with the group disembarked for another star ship and they all went to the 'step off point' where retrieval of people and cargo could take place as a light transfer, these included tubes.

Recimer came in and greeted everyone in the step off point lounge and gave a smile to Renee and an even larger one to Lorenzo. "Ah, Recimer, you can be hard to find around the place", said Lorenzo, meaning he was seemingly pre-occupied with things. Recimer pointed behind him to the step off point tubes, the light then dissipated and who should have arrived but Carlos, Janice, Brine and Dalgorius. Lorenzo and Renee turned to each other and then Recimer, particularly Lorenzo and smiled, he then steadily walked over to his old school and archaeological colleagues. Janice was the first he recognized followed by her brother she had convinced at a later time after the group first left for the ship, his name was William and then the others. "Wow, do I feel old", Lorenzo said as he came over and gave a great hug to all there. "We have had a wonderful time out in the quadrant of space, Lorenzo, there's so much you could see and experience out there", said Janice. "This is my brother William you haven't met as yet and he's doing a form of therapy analysis as he's had a history in medicine", she continued, "he now studies this for a living, this is his goal to learn of this civilization." Brine was doing a form of medical accountancy, for space crew and civilians coming and going from the planets with his brother Dalgorius doing similar study and work. "What about you Carlos, and pretending pulled out a crystal from his pocket rolling back his eye's and putting on a fake deeper tone, "Well, I have been looking into..." the whole group burst out in laughter at his parody of past events from the discovery point at the labyrinth on Earth. At this point Recimer showed up to them, smiling and projected something to them new. It was so that the Henuburian had the psychic abilities stronger than anyone else, Hybrid or Human, though they all possessed it. "Just wanted to show you what it was you were missing", this projection was strange as it seemed familiar but also not so familiar, whilst this projection was taking place, Ismondera appeared and whilst to the group this seemed almost like dejavu before, it also seemed like a projection they almost had to have, like there was an unfinished pattern within their internal dialogue. "Your just doing this to scare us, you tag team", said Lorenzo, "This is part of your preparation" replied Recimer. They had a series of physical projections focused into their minds from the minds of Recimer and Ismondera, some of this was graphically disturbing and made them feel like they were in a slow motion dream, "This is no joke is it Ismondera", projected Brine as they all seem to become more telepathic, projections seem to came in as the information came in and then it stopped abruptly! Only Recimer was present, "What was that about!" gasped Lorenzo. "This is so you know that your growth has not finished, training is a difficult task at times". "What is ....?" and with most of the group of friend's in awe and interest as to what had just taken place as if a demon from the past had grabbed them and shook them up, Recimer continued "The heightening of your evolutionary process can and will take many twists and turns, this will continue to operate for as long as necessary. The second part of your spiritual awaking can occur, I say can, because for some of you as Progenitors, of all of you here can attest to which is the meaning of a progeny in your Earthly language, is why you should wake to what is happening... but one incursion this time, to go further you will have to stay as a Progenitor but in addition a Hybrid will be attached to you for the realms in space open to you, will be open to us. You see it began many millennia ago in the mapping of quadrant A, and this I will commune and communicate no further to you." At this a strange silence fell upon the friends who even after making a reunion after some years were now strangely speechless as they had to make up their minds individually in accepting the terms Recimer the Henuburian set out. "This would mean giving up a journey to quadrant B." Brine reiterated to Janice what they had spoken to them and they all collectively looked at one another as if looking at each other again for the first time and this began the questions both to Recimer and Ismondera to just what exactly what it was they had meant, the Henuburian's but as to what was assumed that to the experiences that were to happen in the mapping journey ahead of them. "Recimer and Ismondera obviously want us to come to a conclusion and you know that this requires some sense of just acceptance" retorted Dalgorius, "Yes we're obviously here for the long haul. The idea of becoming as a hybrid is somewhat alarming, I just did not think this would occur so quickly!" retorted Carlos back. The description of the Hybrid, was in between the Henuburian and the Human in appearance, they were taller but their being was permeated by a strange fluorescence like that of light, the heights of them varied but this was an overall case of their appearance with the exception of some of the Henuburian like Ismondera who had changed his DNA to suit that of humans.

Quadrant A had been the mapping of the first leg of their experience maybe taking that of millions of years to do this one task, settling planets, seeing a planet fall and disintegrate when the location of one planet had expired in terms of age, much time had passed and this had influenced their first operative, directive.

The next decision was to be in the best frame of mind and this Recimer had tried to get across for them to digest so that they understood what was in store for them. The twenty six letter idea of a new alphanumeric system had past and now what was being ensued was the delivery of an understanding of the universe that they were coming into. This required not only the first alphanumeric system but a second mapping/vibration and this with each and every new inhabitant that approached and found in the quadrant they were now in and the whole idea was going to change future outcomes and possibly all their height and growth patterns for those that continues in this, it was something to consider since they were going to be stuck on a star ship for much of their waking lives.

The next thing to occur was that the group split up, they were met by another grouping of the Henuburian and Hybrid emissaries and crew, and they included Matorthus, Ismondera and Manderell, who the latter was a piloteer for the Nop. There was going to be a re-activation of a type of course structure, this course of events required during this trip that a use of materializing and dematerializing factors were to be instigated, this was the second part of the initiation of the friends, that included Micheal from their star ship, his partner Delice, Carlos, Janice, Brine, Dalgorius; Lorenzo and Renee's friends, Sandriea, Dolly, Beaunia and Suiga. They later were led in and reported to the main dispatch area in the step off point lounge and it was from here that the announcement was made from Brine. Brine had a great enthusiasm to go with this idea and to follow this team for where-ever their adventures would take them, "We are to disembark for those of us who wish to go on and not to just flee back to Earth, I personally don't see it as an option. I think we should all be excited about this event and would love to see everyone come along and in the spirit of all the graciousness bestowed upon us from these beings amidst everything that has transpired here and Neru with the combining of two planetary cultures there and on Earth, we should be thankful." All three of the Henuburian were in the background as if anticipating the event to follow and everyone knew something was going on, it was almost certain that the idea to go was strong, strong in all but one, Lorenzo and that followed by Renee!

With all the work and living they had achieved on board was highly regarded by all Henuburian, for all they had, there was still this lingering that it was not in their best interests but as Ismondera saw it, they were old souls and they would come along with just enough coxing. They were a special couple and had inspired many as he and the other Henuburian saw it. And with the nice feelings and knowing of Lorenzo and Renee, this was alright. Brine who from the beginning of things related to their introduction with Ismondera to Neru and to the star ships they transitioned, the CO, Nop and other transport ships, he would try to convince Lorenzo. "We would miss you dearly but even more we would not be the same without you, we need you on our journeys, mate", giving the best wording he knew to keep Lorenzo from slipping away from the group and this was to be the convincing from Brine as he was the best on the ship to get him to come along, this had been actioned by Ismondera for him to do, he continued, "please don't ...don't leave us Lorenzo... it would be so unlike us to continue without you. We've always kept in touch with you and this would not be us then, it would be us without a great and good friend!" Brine implored, Lorenzo looked at the floor and then at Brine, then the group finished looking at Ismondera. Renee placed her hand on Lorenzo's shoulder, "What do you want to do Darling, I'm with you where ever you go, you know that", and Lorenzo grasped her hand in a reassuring gesture. "Look, I have struggled and I suppose right through but if you all are here and one family on this and...", he looked at Ismondera for reassurance, he continued, "and I believe you do, are, then I've..." pausing again and turning to Renee, continuing "We have really no choice but to come with you, we are on this, I'm with you!", they applauded and let out a cheer of celebration and he turned and hugged Renee.

"We have gone through so much, together", implored Brine and Brine turning to Ismondera and the others, shook hands, each with the other and the representatives of the Henuburian's all toasted to the occasion. "We have made it and now we will begin with a toast to Ismondera, Matorthus and others of the Henuburian council including Hybrid and Human crew on board the ships". The beginning of this was a speaker from the council of the Henuburian, to the right of him. All this was psychically sent in audible tones, the Henuburian's chose to send it in the form of physical verbosity and telekinetic or psychic language. This had a predisposition with some of the Human population as this was not readily understood and seemed more like a forced projection into the mind. They did this now as they were the chosen group for the adventurers that lay ahead. It was not noticeable that this was all telepathic projection by the group, especially now as they had come through so much and this only made them listen more intently. There Henuburian language could change its density in meaning depending on who was listening and the circumstances involved with them, the speaker was a Henuburian named Vaale. "We are bringing you into this because we are reaching a time of completion with the work of Quadrant A, now this spills over in the working of the exploration and recording of Quadrant B. The first intelligent variational variants from this region have been composed, it is called Darlapaatha-a. This means the language barrier has

90

been breached and this is the sign and co-sign derivatives of intelligent language derivatives that we now can work from and translate. This translation is part of our protocol as Henuburian's to map the cosmos. This is a time of celebration. Please go into the hall and our group will show you their data variant from the pyramid computer. We each have a set of Progenitors on every star ship, they are Human as on the Nop, the CO which this group was a part. Will you accompany us into the joining of the Progenitors of this ship and we will explore and share and show you around this department", Vaale concluded. The group followed them mainly all being Henuburian, some Hybrid and some Human and all went into the rest of the display area of the computer terminal.

It was demonstrated that the machine that had gathered the information for each ship was connected to all the artefact history that the past Progenitors had gathered going back more than twenty thousand years ago when the Henuburian had been in the Andromeda and Orion star systems and had started their early mapping of 'quadrant A' for many millennia and had derived much of the syllabus of language strewn throughout the galaxies, developing to the further twenty-six variational frequencies of the universal octaves. Each of these octaves were linked to a parallel universe, one that the Henuburian's were aware that if this area was crossed, it would lock into the quadrant A, making the job of mapping time consuming and more complex. To this end they developed a technology to inhibit the progression of the vibration octaves and determining the where and when in the ever present reality of the space of quadrant A. Thus this is carried on through the work of the Progenitors to record and analyse all this work in the mapping. Lorenzo pointed out what there was to be taken into account with the operations with the Progenitors and what they had to accomplish, there was generally some deferment with Micheal as to what was to be important. There had always been issues regarding the process as to what had been placed into the data banks and that this was cause for Ismondera and Matorthus to take issue with them in regards to the computer. The distribution of these around the ship and when they were needed was the next phase to the whole aspect to what there evolvement would thus entail being more responsible. The groups involved would all be put through this in the first phase of inducted star ship training.

Calibrations were made of the computer terminals capacitor, for on this ship, a capacitor was more like an equivalent of a absorbable material with a technological super-skin, an advancement of what they had to offer on the ship was, within was generally an intelligently grown, internal interface to help compute to the best possible advantage of the computer, theses capacitors/transmogriphier with some, sometimes were made of different materials but had the same function, only at different capacities. These were the pyramid computers themselves, some had a crystal arrangement within and some did not. The crystal arrangement had a definite express use for the Henuburian. Not all the information was retrievable because the Henuburian had reasons for believing that this would be used in the wrong way by Human interests with the wrong intent. This however was different for the newly inducted human contingent interest and who were to know what to do with these devices as trained by the Henuburian's.

"Settings have change, Matorthus", Brine suggested who now worked alongside Lorenzo on the Nop. "Why do you believe this to be so?" he replied. "The co-ordinates are not in line with the data input in the pyramid from section five" (or translation in Henuburian 'nire for five). "Nire?" Matorthus replied with impunity. "Yes, it could be the vibration threshold for this area has not been fully calculated yet." The vibration threshold was something to do with the octave, which translated in Henuburian terms, a full complement of the wave or vibration but it looked like it was going to be a sound wave sounding as 'd'. This looked to be so and gradually Brine confirmed it was the sound wave. The first variational construction to understand the quadrant B! This sound wave was then calibrated into data fragments and then resewn into the computer sychometery of the Nop's star ship computer analogue and main frame and for any other ship. This was to be the information to be downloaded to other star ships in the quadrant so as not to create confusion, the Nop was the first one to enter! "Continue the process of system mapping identification, continue heading of system directives", replied Matorthus, now the advisory piloteer for the Nop, was looking out to a flare of red nebula appearing to the right of the visual window. He prompted the head piloteer to the conference lounge near the step off point for retrievals.

Chapter 2. A banding of ships

As the first vibration fragments had been retrieved, the additional ships, starting with the Calla and the Optomiox were to soon make their appearance, followed by a host of others, as these star ships had finished all their work ties with quadrant A, so as to continue in the new unmapped quadrant started by the Nop. The Nop was a dispatch ship to do such a purpose.

Matorthus began to collaborate all who were involved and from this point on, it was imperative that an acute understanding of the personnel on board the ship were accounted for as security was stepped up and the initiation of all now involved was to happen.

The ships to appear included the aforementioned ships, and also Macusulua pronounced Maa cuu suu lua, Verity pronounced Veerie tee, Mobilius CO, and from the squadron of the Eptimo pronounce Eip tee moe and the suspension of Eptimo one through to 10, the Valenquez pronounced Vael een queez and there squadron of ships one through to ten, the Alpenphillior pronounced Aael peen phiel leeor, the Macontuscious a huge scout craft, pronounced Maac oon tusciouus, the Valperria pronounced Vaal peer rie a, The Moccon Tupescia pronounced, Moec con Tuupescie a, and it's squadron of ships one through to ten, The Vaalpetio, a large pyramid ship and it's squadron of ships one through to ten, The Normioon pronounced Noorm ie oon, a massive cylindrical mother ship and it's squadron of twenty ships, the Mobilltenus, Moob iell tenuus, another massive cylindrical ship with a squadron of twenty ships, and about another forty of the cylindrical ships were included each with a squadron of ten ship each, this included another variety of ships, looking more like space Sky freighters or Mool bers, these were craft that were followed by the

Henuburian's because they were causing trouble for some of the planets that were under the protection of the Henuburian's, though were easily identifiable to the Henuburian to be their own as they were more advanced, also included were the saucer shaped craft that the Henuburian had as well, one hundred thousand in all.

They had starting with the Nop capabilities included were the ability of the cylindrical ships, the ability to go invisible and to fold space time (to be in two places at once), some of the scout ships involved with the Pyramid ships, could split into two or more parts for more manoeuvrability, though it wasn't essentially important but particularly in and around asteroids, some of the craft were as old as a thousand years with some made only recently. Multi dimensional capabilities could include ghosting or (diminishment of material crafts body and reintegration). Some believed it for manoeuvres to do with trajectory and avoidance of space debris.
"Trajectory has been set", said Matorthus. The audible languages auditory system had been activated and like a school pa system, the voice, a multi-vibration language, could be heard by all ships auditory, telekinetic and psychic distribution mechanisms.

The voice prompt was integrated with the ships mono log systems, so that the bio-technological Ai systems could participate in the event as well as the voicing over of some of the Henuburian technicians, Hybrids and Humans, in that order. Though it was only the Henuburian that had integrated voice modulation with the computers Ai system on board with their own so that both of them participated in real time! A being by the name of Vaale, initiated the beginning introduction with the computer monolog and Henuburian, "Voice test, integration, welcome planet, planet bodies, star ships, cylindrical, pyramid, amorphic production ships (meaning of typical grid manufacturing of their ships), and saucers all types. Greetings, this is the first point of vibration of a new Quadrant for the second centenary vibration' B'.
A great applaud was heard through all channels of energy frequencies, that meant no matter if it was kinetic, the sound vibration from the applaud from all present, Henuburian, Hybrid and Human could be heard through the sound spectrum, whether physically or psychically. "I now pass this over to Matorthus, head of

Quadrant affairs" and sounding like a microphone being passed over, another applaud and a giggle "Thank you, Welcome my dear friends of the collective of Henuburian council" Another applaud rang out, "We are on the cusp of what has not taken place in four hundred thousand years! What an amazing event to be part of!" yet another applaud. "We have set trajectory for the new sector, correction quadrant!" a small giggle ensued from the listeners, "We are heading and the first letter of the quadrant has been recognized, this vibration will be integrated into our own vocabulary and our computer systems. Each on board computer Ai has this ability to detect all references, and this has been pro-activated just recently with all of our on board star ships. The star ships will be the first issued these vibration monologs, the mapping will be integrated soon!" Another applaud, he continued "May all of us for all our efforts so far be congratulated and the keepers of this system of integration", the speaker Vaale could be heard in the background at this point acknowledging what Matorthus just mentioned, he continued, "And we should do some celebrating, mindfully mind you," giggles rang out again, again continuing, "to this one in four-hundred thousand year event, please give yourself an applaud... and thank yourselves", "I will now pass this onto Lorenzo and Renee and Micheal and Delice. Again the microphone sound, another giggle from the listeners, "We are pleased", said Micheal, "yes please" Lorenzo pitched in, Micheal continued, "to be a part of this moment with you in you, the Henuburian history", a slight giggle rang out again, he continued, "our interpretations of your world and ours is noted in Neru of which we participated when we joined you, and gladly we participated! The whole idea of doing this was so in ground in me, I felt chosen to do this very task!" "Eh hem!" voiced Lorenzo and another applaud and laughter rang out, continuing again. "Lorenzo, I love you! We and our wives and particularly without our wives this would not have been possible for us to do, so you can tell, I now pass this onto Lorenzo, who will finish of my words and thank you!" "Yes thank you, Micheal, the alphabet symbolism would have a whole new range of interpretation. For instance 'a' could mean 'ah' in vibration, c could be 'Cu' and yet represent another symbol altogether. The interpretation could be the same for the beings of the quadrant 'B' universe as opposed to the quadrant 'A'.

Chapter 3. The presage and procedure

"Events had occurred, Micheal and Delice were given to understand that a vibration throughout the ship had occurred, they were called to the lounge area of the ship to witness along with Brine and Janice a strange phenomenon occurring. The window holographic display came up on the hull as the ship had numerous cell points to enable visual viewing from the material hulls of their star ships." It is magnificent" said Delice to the Henuburian now, council present, a plasma type nebula of a nature that had not been seen if ever in the regular 'quadrant A' was seen to be occurring with more frequent regularity. "We have picked up transmissions, they are being relayed to the analogue readers of our Ai computer, these appear and disappear at will, at least most of them and seem to be the source of our contact", reported Locor, one of the piloteers for the ship. Manderell, Ismondera, Matorthus and Ismondera made up part of the Henuburian council on the Nop.

"Text had been received directly from the nebula as this cloud of space gases began to fluctuate wildly with light with a slight audible tone frequency translating the same message. "Your presence here is an act of war", then the cloudy nebula vanished as quickly as it had come. The Henuburian council consulted and wanted to know what Micheal and Delice thought of the spectacle. "We believe ourselves that it was not from here this quadrant and assisting a source other than here as well", said Matorthus. "My assumption be it right or wrong is that it was possibly from a sky freighter Molbers (Moolbers)" "And we've thought this too but the thread from which it came went straight to this quadrant B and not to any Molbers ship," said Micheal. "Could it be that we are at a crossroads with this universal energy here" replied Delice, Just then Lorenzo and Renee walked through the partition sliders. "We heard, from one of the elders, Galmeda", mentioned Renee, "As you've been upgraded in your position here from the co-alliance you previously had with the 'Job', you all have a knowledge of the work we are doing now, I mean it was either here on this star ship or back to Earth, again, I'm glad you chose us because look at what your witnessing", enthused Matorthus. "I'm proud to have you all on board, simply

96

because you had the personality to stick with us, there is also another message from these other beings that I also detect, it's one of relief that we have arrived" "Yes, they are from the same source point vibration, though we haven't determined if they are from the same planetary alliance." replied Locor.

Members of the Hybrid, knew all of the information of the Henuburian council and were more in advanced training and understanding of the ship usages, it was usually up to them through the Henuburian's when to interpret the new beings coming on to a ship and their planetary understanding. Members of the Hybrids Humans, came in to the lounge and helped with a further understanding of who they were and their past. The Henuburian council understood this and the emotion attached to them. "All the ships have stationed themselves according to the ship Ai computer factors. We have a bearing North toward, what is called Buicce sector, these will be the first of many sectors to explore, once the vibration pattern has been exemplified, uploaded onto the analogue computers", counselled Matorthus, to both the Human and Hybrid Human groups.

Chapter 4. Disaster strikes

A flash ensued on the side of the ship CO. It surprised and created a type of paralysis in all that had experienced it. What had ensued had been picked up on the computers by piloteer, Nevenotec, (Sadlopap), which was a ship analogue data language of protocol and procedure used by all the ship computers.

The pilots sat at their consoles of the CO, Vyane Deport and Nevenote Tenniol Beel. "All that I can report is that Nevenotec has precluded an anomaly, which is being run through all possible outcome on all ship analogue, Vaale has moderate to most control over that and we should get answer", he paused, "Here it is through Sadlopap and it presumes that the closest possibility was the communication dispersion used by our data link communication to other worlds and ships", replying this to Vyane."Yes, it would seem that this has been a problem for us previously but we have undergone a transit into another uncharted territory of space, the odds of this happening is more increased, we should report this soon, to all crew on the ship", said Vyane,. "It's only a matter of time that this could be used as an initiative of possible infiltration into the ship analogue data banks." Nevenotec replied back "Announcement, repeat announcement", came from the prompter from Vaale, one of the operators on board, this went through all the forty thousand ships in the space contingent of the mapping of Quadrant B. Darlapaatha-a. "The ship CO, have suffered a rare attack of space radiation from a presumed source, a sky freighter or Moobel contingent. Please watch for this anomaly physically and through Sadlopap data streams, there is a transition of older quadrant data A to quadrant data B that is taking place and being reviewed and updated from now on until this has been fully reviewed and done, note, there will be revision in language encodement on ships computers. There is the growing threat of another of these radiation attacks, some hospitalization has taken place from the CO, all have been exposed but are recovering, thank you all for your attention!", after Vaale had finished saying these things and lifted his finger from the pilots consul he turned to Matorthus, Vyan and Nevenotec. "This is quite a serious event and great care has to be taken by all crew. We must regard the ships computers as going through transition themselves, dialogue and number letter function has transited in its own way, shielding ratio's vibrational equipment will be monitored and adjusted" Gelicoda!, this is not Gelicoda, not again.." hissed Matorthus, Gelicoda, represented language and the coding of it, not only for ships main system frames Ai but the vocabulary would have more words added. "Yes, yes I know, but we haven't done this in a while", Vaale now grinning, "A long while!" pausing and looking at all of them concerned, "Don't worry, synchronization will be only a small transition" Gelicoda, that's going to be a lot of adjusting...oh well!", replied Vyan. Nevenotec and Matorthus just smiled.

Now around the ship and through them, data streams were sourced, now they continued to be until they had no more information to collect from the etheric space vibrations around them. The mapping was presumably completed, this was not until the mapping, language and architectural vibrations had been synchronized and updated with quadrant A to quadrant B. Information and upgrades. It proved to effect ship mechanism and structures through the ships, the Henuburian language had extra words added, once these were determined and complete on the ships, the dialogue would prove full mapping had completed. From there, the approach of worlds could be acceptable to the host quadrant. Darlapaatha-a, would be the new home of the Progenitors, Henuburian, Hybrids Progenitors and Human/Progenitors. volunteers to do this. Ai technician for the Nop, Vaale and the Hybrid, a security personnel member for the CO, whose name was Kareetle It wasn't usual practice to send any newly recruited beings to do the work of exploration of any planetoid. The appearance of the Nop came close to the foundry, this is the planet first named and remained to be a mystery to all those on the ship, although he Henuburian had a knowledge of the planets geometry geography.

The two of them left the step off lounge and went on to flash down to the surface and had found their co-ordinates had shifted slightly to what they projected to. "Our settings have changed, it must be a Delphenian planet (A Delphenian planet was generally a high technology expected planet and could take on illusion.) The group that had left off from their spot had found a chamber ahead." "And there is the appearance of a sealed door ahead, Matorthus?" said Kareetle. The co-ordinates are 52.5 longitudes by 80.6 latitude" "You're reading must be distorted", said Matorthus. "It keeps moving one or two points" replied Vaale. "Just keep a watch out for any surprises, we suspect what you are thinking, we'll keep you informed" "Thank you Matorthus and Vaale", both said in unison. "Now we could have a problem, the co-ordinates keep changing and yet the cloud (nebula) has led us here, I think there is more to this cloud than we first thought," continued Matorthus "I agree", said Ismondera, "We are already surmising a possible sabotage of our team..." he paused. Increase the scanner projection, it might uncover the layers of the problem that is causing the problem in the structures surrounding the co-ordinates and therefore an extraction may be better to accomplish," Matorthus said sternly. "I agree with that," replied Ismondera. "We'll pull them out now then" Beams were focused on all possible co-ordinates of their arrival on the planet. A white beam began to appear from the intensity of the energy and usually Henuburian protocol was over ridden to extract their team. "Wait, it's not the surround co-ordinates, its whatever is in the chamber ahead" said Matorthus, "It's isolated from the step off beam, we can light step (another term for beaming up) them up no problem then" replied Vaale, "Yes, it highly probable there is nothing to worry or be concerned about" said Ismondera. "Can you scan within the structures of the door and the room, whatever is interfering with your co-ordinate location is nothing to do with our equipment, it's in your equipment" "Alright, Matorthus, we'll proceed with the scanning" Kareetle began the scan, "It's got subtle movement", said Kareetle. At this point too, one more from the Nop flashed down and one specialist in the field of new life forms from the star ship, Moccon Tupescia, a Henuburian by the name of Gaaddel and a Hybrid named Murial.

"Glad to see more help from the crew" said Vaale. "We're needing to know what's really in there", said Kareetle. "And that's why we're here, I can tell by the doors this is to do with a civilization with high technological function. They are penetrable but there is a reading or two we have to take to find out what it really is and what its functions are, unlike ourselves just guessing", Gaaddel replied, and peering at the scanning device of the slate computer, he responded confirming from the data he had already received, "They are Techno bots of some kind obviously but without taking an in room investigation, we won't know....fully", he said "That's what we thought, technological robots, our scan has demonstrated kinetic, audio functions and wave energy demonstrating that", replied Vaale.

Gaaddel focused on the doors and he moved almost stealthily to the doors. His personal log of information had Vaale and Kareetle guessing. Murial walked over and took readings off the doors. Gaaddel waved over to Murial to take a look at the bottom section of door. His isotopic reading flash incessantly as if an opening had been found. "It a low amplification and it reads all equipment near it. This will be our way in and if a warning is to occur, this will be the way to read it and if necessary, our way back out!" he paused, "Force field active." And the delivery system went into synch with their equipment, all force field were active. The sound treatment began and the Ai manifestation of the two half circle doors activated.

A dim whispery sound began and the doors parted rather quickly. As they all walked in what came into view showed to be a myriad of metal grey cylindrical enclosures on pale beings with dark to light hair in a state of stasis. A laser light atop of the ceiling circled the top of the room and was presumed to be surveillance, although their instrumentation showed it to be benign to this. Ai manifestations of the two half circle doors were activated, Muriel and Kareetle ran over but they closed. "Don't worry, we are fully protected!" replied Gaaddel, A metallic clink was heard as they closed, the door was shut "Yes, we should not want this to be our tomb," said Vaale, engaging with the Nop and testing electron gadgetry in his vestment robe and strobing all the light functions in it. "Test all electron rig sets, crew!", said Gaaddel, (these being defense analogue technology in their clothing) Peeps beeps and whistles started to be broadcast from them all, Gaaddel continued, "Diplomacy, crew, keep tight. We aren't here to spill any life force..." Vaale interrupted Gaaddel. "Yes but we are also into self preservation, be careful but if you have to" and turning looking directly at Gaaddel, "if any life force is spilled, then it won't be our own! There are medics on board our ships," Vaale finished saying. "Yes..." replied Gaaddel. A loud din and a fusion reaction took place, activating a secondary function, that awoke a whole set of the being that had lain dormant. Bleeps whistles and peeps could be heard as defensive measures were enacted by the crew and stepping back from the metallic cylinders the beings were in.

Chapter 5. Rapture

There was the decision that the whole adventure undertaken would be catalogued, recorded and paged back to all associate civilizations of the Henuburian, that they had undertaken through objectives given the follow up parameters of people like those on the Progenitors project set by the Henuburian and this was to change and re-adapt to different environments with which space had provided for the ships and themselves, to read and at the end of it all, this was the best determination of thought that was the follow up of Henuburian logic and thought. It accounted to a philosophy that they can either regress or reassessing their objectiveness with what they were doing, this in reading the vibrations of space and supposedly to pre-determine to others, sources of logic and thinking through this, even tightening on

101

the security of what they were doing at this time. This was a type of distraction that was needed if they were to further follow into the outer reaches of the universe to explore the rapture of it all.

There had been previous upheavals in the Henuburian civilization but these had practically smoothed out by space travel. The parameters of their ships and themselves were the guidance for their civilizations on the planets they lived on and ones they helped.

Chapter 6. Irreconcilable logic

The journey had commenced without incidence and now there were certain space upheavals. These were to be expected as they had commenced with new mapping area of the cosmos that were only monitored through instrumentation and now was physical as if through a doorway being explored. "The allowable range was contextually for at least ten quasars distance, this equated to trillions of light year miles", Matorthus postulated to the group with him but erred to Ismondera in particular about this. It had been well and truly in their data texts for at least fourteen thousand years but they had to update those records.

Curiously they had no reproach with the idea of salient ideology which was rather cool and calm in the idea of a God in the universe, for that was to be understood from their perspective to be from another realm and yet of the universe itself. Yet all their text data had tracts pertaining to this idea and the source was from a mysterious one.

The Progenitors transit flashed aboard from the Alpenphillior star ship as they had been on tours through the ships with the Progenitors as to understanding of ship interface with other Ai computers on board and now to one of the main cylindrical ships, called the Normioon. Ismondera continued to read the fourteen thousand year text data, "You are to be reaching toward this parameter and this is your quadrant", again Matorthus postulated looking at Ismondera as if for guidance, he continued, "Your station is found derived and led?" Ismondera motion to the control panel. "Matorthus looked at Ismondera with eyes of impediment, intense, Ismondera's eyes provoked a response from the hyper-capacitors on the panel and began an intense interface with the Ai computer. Concerned, Matorthus motioned to Ismondera's hand and so he could see his finger and then the outside of the ship. Pointing, Matorthus made light of the fact that a strange glow pervaded the outside of the hull of the Normioon, the glow intensified and seemed to be in the direction of the Nop star ship. Ismondera gather everyone quickly, "What is it?" replied Matorthus but realizing as soon as Ismondera looked at him once more, they realizing something was happening, fled to the flash tube of the step off lounge of the Normioon.

In an instant, they were back in record time to the CO ship, Ismondera quickly made his way to the area of the ship where it had its incident and sure enough an all pervading glow had begun, taking place outside of it. "It's a message", Ismondera briefly uttered to Matorthus, now more of the ships council and members of the Hybrids and Henuburian's of the ship were crowding, Vaale had been with them, Give this to me now Vaale". It was the projection wand for the Ai's, Ismondera focused the thought form from the collective information of the ships Ai's at the wand and tuned it into all the ship analogues, "No Ismondera, not at it" He veered it off centre from the light field emanating on that port side of the CO. Everyone began to stand back away from the beam projection from Ismondera and also the light. A change began to occur, as a colouration began to pervade it, pinks mauve and blue, some quite intense, it then began to move back and out from the ship but staying out from the ship. Then Ismondera quickly activated the wand on the CO's ship's Ai pyramid, starting from the top of it to the base, the aura from the emanation had pervaded the wand. "Be careful Ismondera", Vaale warned him. This hasn't happened in fourteen thousand years", mentioned Vaale. The pyramid began to beam blue, and then the transfer box next to it glittered with different colours, intently. The download was projected into all Ai computers now, all ships transferred instantly the language that had been transmitted. Some rocking of the ships could be felt as was normal with sufficient downloads of information. The translation began, the language barrier had been reached and a block removed. It read, "Here, all well come e you are here to be of assistance to our worlds, translation of text data complete..." "A great cheer was felt on all levels and a guided pathway was presented to the ship, for the first world to receive assistance from the CO and others. The Nop came into view followed by all their other ships, one hundred thousand of them pulled into view.

Ismondera, was then followed in by all the Progenitors and who was with them at the time Lorenzo and Renee, Micheal and Delice, Suiga, Dolly.... "How did you know Ismondera?" said Suiga, and looking at Matorthus, then Renee and Lorenzo, spoke seemingly out of character, "I don't know, it was just a hunch.", and smiled, they all smiled back but it was a chorus of cheers that could be heard throughout all the star ships, all the people who had been effected by the source nebula had virtual recovered fully.

"This is the culmination of what took place back in Neru after the time vault!" Suggested Lorenzo, he continued, "Yes it was as if the aliens had told us about ourselves, again" he gesture as if rolling his eyes. They continued to look at the Nebulous light as it appeared now having departed from the CO, the path and co-ordinates were clear.

Back on the Nop, they found that all the relevant data had changed but was the last ship to do so. "CO, this is Caleberel, I'd like to speak with Ismondera." "What is it, Caleberel? Not anything to do with the anomaly outside your ship?" No, but the information has been the last to translate on this ship, what is your idea on this?" "It's just a thought form reading, probably from the Nebula itself, nothing to worry about, just data base it into the analogue" replied Ismondera, "Done...and well done Caleberel" "Thank you, Ismondera, he replied"

"This shock wave of events has taken everybody by surprise, it's not the first time for things like this to happen this way but we have to be on the ready, ready act out when this happens," said Ismondera. "We've now got the message", Matorthus grandly suggested back. "All the occupants are now being led but still we're monitoring the anomaly where it takes us" Vaale said. "The planet, if indeed it is a planet, where is it leading? I mean what are the co-ordinates now? Our translation has almost completed and the whole numerical grid should be understandable with our newly translated language. We can only suggest by older records, that it's the vibrational system translated by the collective Ai to be Vahnlarpaa", replied Matorthus "Vahnlarpaa?" repeated Matorthus stroking his chin, he continued "Give us a frame work overlay of this Quadrant B with Quadrant A", "How is this supposed to have anything to do with this nebula and the expected planet Matorthus. "Just trust me on this" he replied. Immediately Ismondera initiated the readout overlay. "It doesn't look too ambiguous", said Vaale looking over his shoulder at the flat holographic display. "Constellation Lyra coincides with this, that interesting, see this pocket here next to the tail of Lyra, we have a collection of stars somewhere in here is our forefront of confrontations with the Molbers, sky freighters." What are you suggesting Matorthus" Ismondera said sternly. "This area could be...we're being followed", he paused, walked over to the consoles in the rear of the room doing a site check through master command of all areas of most of the ships", Do a site sweep check on the Macusulua and make a group of two of us and three Progenitors comes with us, he said sternly. This was one of their ships in the fleet. They immediately made way to the step off lounge through to the Macusulua. Head piloteer made his way to the group when they came out of the light tubes. Gamtreepl, so glad to see you, how are the passengers" saying this is an almost bowing posture as the piloteers were sometimes postured to do. "We have a query and a suspicion, though highly unlikely, that there is a possible infiltration of the ship command, which we ask, would you object to a scanner search of the immediate areas of the ship without informing through immediate communication channels, as is usual." "This is unusual, though at this time it is not totally permissible as a language readjustment of all settings through the language interference we had has beset the ship..." he stopped Gamtreepl in mid sentence. "No, you'll have to do this for us, remember the Nop is one of the head Progenitor ships operating, scans and all, may I remind you, we do have the final say!" Gamtreepl, was stunned," well...I" He immediately became disoriented and went to reach for a shock gun and a peal rang out as the gun discharged. "I thought you were the piloteer.. Oh well" said Matorthus as he turned to Ismondera. Their devices were on the highest levels, "Obviously something wrong with the captain, who else is infected" It just occurred to me, was not the nebula intersected by you on this ship" "So..." Ismondera paused as he looked at Matorthus, "But of course, this whole notion that the consoles were invariably problematic...the transition of languages engaged the ships mainly and namely these one's" Ismondera agreed. They continued through to the piloteers quarters and notified senior and security personnel for the investigation. Murial, Kareetle, please secure these areas" these were the piloteers and adjoining Matorthus continued, " we'll investigate the rest of the ship", moving off whist taking along other of the senior protectorate of the ship, fifteen in all. They headed toward the North East wing of the ship and found a door to be inoperable. "It won't slide, dematerialize or anything" It's been tampered with, Ismondera concluded. Out came the shock gun, settings were loaded to vibration scan of the door, "Scanning.. it won't budge." Ismondera concluded, "There's Molber in there, quick!" said Matorthus. "Get ready" The shock gun went into destruct mode disintegrating the door permanently, creating a thunder clap of sound "Molber! Mol...," shouted Matorthus and others of the security, two figures identified by their outfits and stature quickly departed through with stolen technology and through a crackling opening of energy. "Yenod ta bara, translated, our language has come with surprises" said Sepre, one of the personnel of the ship who also accompanied them, "Yes, it's true, let's hope that the last of the problems due to the cloud, meaning the nebula" Matorthus retorted. "It went from the Nop permanently, I can assure you." said Ismondera. The disorientation level from the departure point of the Molbers in the room was being ascertained by Ismondera, through a seismogram energy reader. "No way of following them through, it's got a high disorientation field." Tracking analogue suggested Theloon, another of their personnel. Monitor everyone aboard this ship put the step off lounge in lock down. "no one without proper authorization is allowed on board either" Matorthus firmly predetermined. "Right, will be done" All lock downs were put into place and a search scan of all personnel including security was put into review. The captain piloteer was quarantined to determine his state.

Chapter 7. Questions and answers

106

The area had been sealed off to all other ship with personnel and Ismondera and Matorthus heading the search scan of any infection. Meanwhile Matorthus headed to the sickbay to determine the state of the head piloteer and to see he wasn't lying and to see if he was really who he was! "Gamtreepl, are you awake ", said Matorthus sternly but in a concern. "Where are the Molbers now?" I don't know, what Molbers?" "Where did you get the shock gun, they were banned five hundred years ago, a vintage I admit but dangerous energy if used in the wrong hands... we had to blast a door in the ship with this heinous weapon" "Why did you not use mind coherences to open the door" Gamtreepl replied. They obviously know some of the technology of the ship, catalogued the missing equipment but that won't stop them from using that at a later time? You think?" questioned Matorthus. "They can only use it if there is a problem with the cataloguing, if something is missed" Gamtreepl, we've got this situation in hand, cataloguing and all...they obviously abused you, what did they do Gamtreepl?".He proceeded to cough, then cleared his throat "They apprehended my transmission right after the nebula hit the ship, then through the instrumentation they came through" Who Gamtreepl, who?" retorted Matorthus. Flinching back a wheezing cough, "It was the Molber, two of them ...it was awful, they paralysed me and then got me to do what they wanted...I, that's it" "That's good, you rest now, everything is in hand Gamtreepl" Matorthus got up from the Gamtreepl's lounge sleeper and went to report this to the council. Walking studiously through after ascending one level, Matorthus came into contact with Micheal who had come aboard the CO from the Nop and had listened to report readings from others ships from the console of the CO regarding the incident back at the Nop. "Matorthus, a matter of great urgency has occurred with the pyramid aboard the Nop", he said with haste, Harkening to Micheal's call he twitched his composure and intent to listen. "The pyramid is going into some sort of flux of light with high radiation readings and not just with the Nop, the Eptimo, the Mobilius, Mobilltennus and the Vaalpetio" "Just monitor and put into high security alert status position but this is more than likely a transitional effect of the information additions to the language capacitating. I have pressing matters with the piloteer of the CO at the moment" "What happened?" questioned Micheal. "It would seem we have been infiltrated by Molbers, two of them" "Two of them, what does this mean?" Don't be worried by this as yet, it has been contained", Matorthus smiled as he walked on with Micheal. Just list all the details into the information log analogue system, please." "Yes I'll do just this, I hope this stays contained and that the ship is alright." "There's a source of uncertainty regarding this... don't be concerned" At this Micheal parted from Matorthus. Matorthus entered in the piloteers quarters and spoke with many of the council that were present" "We have a testimony from the head piloteer of this ship and he was only controlled..."pausing, he looked at Murial and Kareetle some of the security personnel, "Is all that equipment in the log vaults recorded?" "Yes, under log in two hundred and three", said Kareetle. Matorthus perused the console and read all the details "One variance pedometer (used for calculating earth gravitational fields, one nelb tube with overlay, (a scribing/reading device used for complex planetary readings) one crystal variance modulator, (this was used for examining tone waves in a predetermined area of space, and one caliber variance examiner, (used for measuring any auditory, and visual readings)". "Yes, they pretty well determined what they wanted and what we did not want them to have. However the prescribed physics is to rely on our own technology and the language the cloud (nebula) has given us, the language has its own encoding anyway."

Micheal the pyramids and Ai's have begun to work down and the light fluctuations and radiation levels have begun to ease, Matorthus Ismondera and all of the group decided to depart from the CO, as all the readings and assessment had been done. Head piloteer, Gamtreepl came with them to the Nop.

All personnel except for Gamtreepl from the Nop came back onto the Nop, "Sigh...this has been a negative turn of events but the pyramids seem to be holding balance, colouration and subtle fluctuations in the line of sight appear steady. (line of sight was the grid work of the Ai pyramids and data retrieval boxes with reports from the Progenitor seemingly back to normal functions with the indicating positive established positron function within the ship data information storage), "we can be certain now that the new additions to the language has been absorbed within these and start real questing with Quadrant B...as was the whole reason to continue this journey!" inflecting almost exasperation, "you understand, Micheal, Lorenzo?" "I only wish one thing" said Lorenzo. "What's that Lorenzo" inflected Matorthus, "That we are heading toward a land of milk and honey" Matorthus looked at a now gazing Ismondera at the window of the ship looking directly out onto the nebula cloud in the deep reaches of space. This time a beautiful purple and orange multi spectrum colouration glow pervading it. "Yes Lorenzo, yes, we are heading for that land of milk and honey", at that Matorthus picked up a slate computer and using calculations and immediately showed them to Renee and Lorenzo and then Micheal and Delice "Twenty six point five, thousand miles away....not far to go", said Matorthus. A crowd had grown and all were looking out through the window at the spectacle.

Chapter 8. Touchdown and final resonance

The impassive and deliberate attempts to control the emotion and anticipation of the first drop off flash down and who would go first was obviously the ire of the moment, with them all being so near to the epicenter of the first contact of the Quadrant B and its new environment would have for them. A transmission signal increased and became a coherent message for the ships Ai. "Approach to...to.... Darlapaatha, transmission out!" Immediately the crew, particularly the piloteers engaged further information from the Ai transmission", "Checking all Sadlopap data streams, for further information regarding third major transmission from the cloud" (nebula). "Nothing further has come through but we have a beacon and co-ordinates matched through the cloud, we have a small planetoid, repeat, small planetoid" Vaale responded. (This is where the first signals of transmissions were related from the cloud). It was soon decided the first of the recipients to go down there and were the first assigned volunteers to do this. Ai technician for the Nop, Vaale and the Hybrid, a security personnel member for the CO, whose name was Kareetle It wasn't usual practice to send any newly recruited beings to do the work of exploration of any planetoid.

The appearance of the Nop came close to the foundry, this is the planet first named and remained to be a mystery to all those on the ship, although he Henuburian had a knowledge of the planets geometry geography.

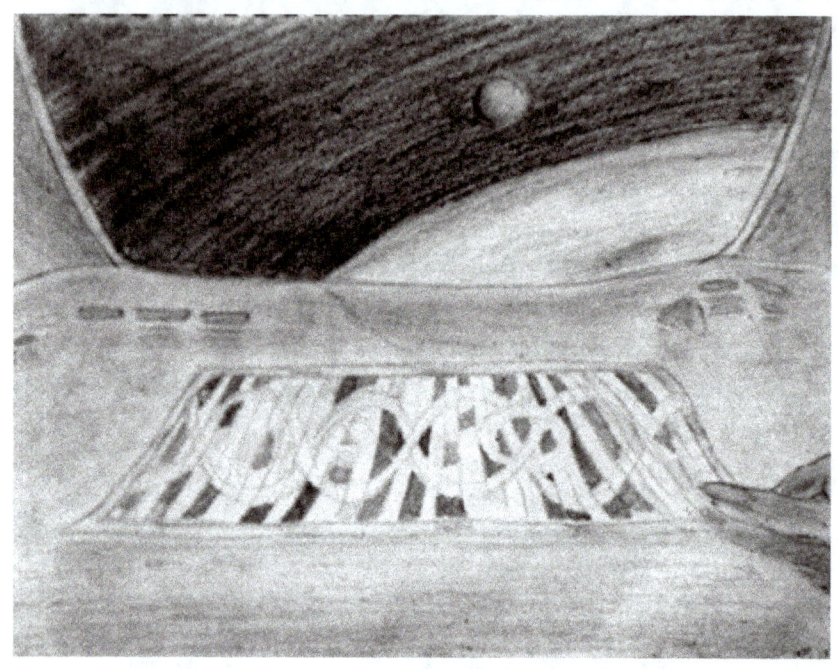

The two of them left the step off lounge and went on to flash down to the surface
and had found their co-ordinates had shifted slightly to what they projected to. "Our
settings have changed, it must be a Delphenian planet (A Delphenian planet was
generally a high technology expected planet and could take on illusion.) The group
that had left off from their spot had found a chamber ahead." "And there is the
appearance of a sealed door ahead, Matorthus?" said Kareetle. The co-ordinates are
52.5 longitudes by 80.6 latitude" "You're reading must be distorted", said Matorthus.
"It keeps moving one or two points" replied Vaale. "Just keep a watch out for any
surprises, we suspect what you are thinking, we'll keep you informed" "Thank you
Matorthus", both said in unison. "Now we could have a problem, the co-ordinates
keep changing and yet the cloud (nebula) has led us here, I think there is more to
this cloud than we first thought," continued Matorthus "I agree", said Ismondera, "We
are already surmising a possible sabotage of our team..." he paused. Increase the
scanner projection, it might uncover the layers of the problem that is causing the

problem in the structures surrounding the co-ordinates and therefore an extraction may be better to accomplish," Matorthus said sternly. "I agree with that," replied Ismondera. "We'll pull them out now then" Beams were focused on all possible co-ordinates of their arrival on the planet. A white beam began to appear from the intensity of the energy and usually Henuburian protocol was over ridden to extract their team. "Wait, it's not the surround co-ordinates, its whatever is in the chamber ahead" said Matorthus, "It's isolated from the step off beam, we can light step (another term for beaming up) them up no problem then" replied Vaale, "Yes, it highly probable there is nothing to worry or be concerned about" said Ismondera. "Can you scan within the structures of the door and the room, whatever is interfering with your co-ordinate location is nothing to do with our equipment, it's in your equipment" "Alright, Matorthus, we'll proceed with the scanning" Kareetle began the scan, "It's got subtle movement", said Kareetle. At this point too, one more from the Nop flashed down and one specialist in the field of new life forms from the star ship, Moccon Tupescia, a Henuburian by the name of Gaaddel and a Hybrid named Murial.

"Glad to see more help from the crew" said Vaale. "We're needing to know what's really in there", said Kareetle. "And that's why we're here, I can tell by the doors this is to do with a civilization with high technological function. They are penetrable but there is a reading or two we have to take to find out what it really is and what its functions are, unlike ourselves just guessing, Gaaddel replied "And peering at the scanning device of the slate computer, he responded confirming from the data he had already received, "They are Techno bots of some kind obviously but without taking an in room investigation, we won't know....fully", he said "That's what we thought, technological robots, our scan has demonstrated kinetic, audio functions and wave energy demonstrating that", replied Vaale.

Gaaddel focused on the doors and he moved almost stealthily to the doors. His personal log of information had Vaale and Kareetle guessing. Murial walked over and took readings off the doors. Gaaddel waved over to Murial to take a look at the bottom section of door. His isotopic reading flash incessantly as if an opening had been found. "It a low amplification and it reads all equipment near it. This will be our way in and if a warning is to occur, this will be the way to read it and if necessary, our way back out!" he paused, "Force field active." And the delivery system went into synch with their equipment, all force field were active. The sound treatment began and the Ai manifestation of the two half circle doors activated.

A dim whispery sound began and the doors parted rather quickly. As they all walked in what came into view showed to be a myriad of metal grey cylindrical

enclosures on pale beings with dark to light hair in a state of stasis. A laser light atop of the ceiling circled the top of the room and was presumed to be surveillance, although their instrumentation showed it to be benign to this. Ai manifestations of the two half circle doors were activated, Muriel and Kareetle ran over but they closed. "Don't worry, we are fully protected!" replied Gaaddel, A metallic clink was heard as they closed, the door was shut "Yes, we should not want this to be our tomb," said Vaale, engaging with the Nop and testing electron gadgetry in his vestment robe and strobing all the light functions in it. "Test all electron rig sets, crew!" Vaale continued (these being defense analogue technology in their clothing). Peeps beeps and whistles started to be broadcast from them all. "Diplomacy, crew, keep tight. We aren't here to spill any life force..." Vaale interrupted Gaaddel. "Yes but we are also into self preservation, be careful but if you have to" and turning looking directly at Gaaddel, "if any life force is spilled, then it won't be our own! There are medics on board our ships," Vaale finished saying. "Yes..." replied Gaaddel. A loud din and a fusion reaction took place, activating a secondary function, that awoke a whole set of the being that had lain dormant. Bleeps whistles and peeps could be heard as defensive measures were enacted by the crew and stepping back from the metallic cylinders the beings were in.

Chapter 9. Interaction

"Awaiting details, Vaale!...Kareetle", said Matorthus and the same follow up was coming from the head piloteer, named Magmadarin from Moccon Tupescia star ship. "Come in please, Gaaddel, Muriel"

The first being spoke, a partitioned language that was not unlike, but different to the Henuburian language they had recently received. The added language enabled the cross layering alphabetical understanding of the Quadrant A to Quadrant B exploration. These beings were the enablers of the Henuburian Hybrid and Human host in helping to reveal the Quadrant they were now in and of the action of exploring and with the Henuburian ancient texts, proved the nebula was the originator of this, the function of the geometric symbol of these circular doors. They would continue from that day forth to work with a new society of alien beings, The Encri.

~~~~

End of book III

Glossary of contents

Inclusive of the glossary of content of characters, events places and things, included within the Time Vault series book; Time Vault, Book I; New Hybrid Colony, Book II; On approach to Darlapaatha-a, Book III. Here is the glossary as follows:

Time Vault: The alien Labyrinth of the Grecian township of
Kalambaka, hosted by Recimer.
Lorenzo is the son of a retired olive plantation owner/part time archaeologist and heads a group of amateur archaeologists to discover the legendary Time Vault.
Renee, wife and partner of Lorenzo, who remained believing of the expeditions to the Time Vault and ultimately the planet Neru, home of the Henuburian.
Lumina, sister of Lorenzo. Markus and Tobias, brothers of Lorenzo.
Lorenzo's companions included his school friend's Carlos, Janice, Brine and Dalgorius, who were part of the amateur group of archaeologists.
Purple crystal, used to convey the message through Carlos to the rest of the group about the Labyrinth.
Hexagonal object, produced holographic image of Recimer, their host alien.
Glass tubes, used for light transportation to Henuburian star ships.
Onlio, Lorenzo's father, who had knowledge on the Time Vault.
Dark crystal used by his father now passed to his son for finding the other Labyrinth door.
Marcie, the Grandmother, who lived in who gave faith to Renee to continued with Lorenzo. Inspector Manos, head detective that followed the trail of Lorenzo.
Agents Fasculus of Interpol and Rogius, who followed the same leads.
S8 team, a division of a security team helping in follow the leads to the Labyrinth.
Neru, Henuburian planet. Captain
Dennis and Commander Fielding of S8 team, searched for Lorenzo and Neru.

Biospherical, some spaceships/craft had this geometric language in describing their ships when translated.

Sychometery, the computer fragments of interaction, put into sync.

Piloteer, one who would steer and/or fly their Henuburian ships.

Enrapturement; the rapture of the moment.

One variance pedometer (used for calculating earth gravitational fields, one nelb tube with overlay, (a scribing/ reading device used for complex planetary readings) one crystal variance modulator, (this was used for examining tone waves in a predetermined area of space, and one calibre variance examiner, (used for measuring any auditory, and visual readings)".

~~~~

Thank you for reading my book, if you want further information and updates, please write to the author at the following address; Nick Betar, c/o Australia Fair post office, Australia Fair, Qld 4215 Australia.

####